Jaxon's Fate

Dawn Love

Dawn Love

Copyright © 2024 by Dawn Love

All rights reserved.

The characters and events portrayed in this book are fictitious. Any similarity to real persons, living or dead, is coincidental and not intended by the author.

No part of this book may be reproduced, or stored in a retrieval system, or transmitted in any form or by any means, electronic, mechanical, photocopying, recording, or otherwise, without express written permission of the publisher.

Photographer: FuriousFotog

Cover Model: Scott Benton

Cover Design: CT Cover Designs

What to Know Before You Read

If you are a reader who doesn't feel the need to be aware of potentially triggering situations in your books, please skip ahead to the next page. If, however, you need to make sure your mental health isn't affected, please read the following statement.

Jaxon's Fate is meant for adults and contains adult situations with explicit and graphic sexual scenes, language, and alcohol use. There is also mention of emotional abuse and parental neglect. It is this author's intent to never cause harm or distress with her words. If ever you feel that there should be a warning about any subject or scene in her work that isn't listed within these warnings, please reach out to her through her social media or email.

dawnloveofficial@gmail.com

Stance on Generative AI

No part of this book has been knowingly created by generative AI. It is this author's stance that generative AI is detrimental to human creativity and hurts human artists and their endeavors. As such, no part of any of her work - writing, photography, narrating, cover design, editing, proofreading, illustrating, or any other service, will be knowingly crafted by generative AI. This author only uses creators she trusts to have and put forth the same values with their work. If, however, some portion of the work she has hired out is ever found to have been created by using generative AI at any time, she will do everything within her power to immediately make corrections and re-hire her work out to other service providers with the same ethical values she holds.

To all of you who spent your formative years doing what was expected and being who you were told to be when it:

Went against everything you wanted.

Went against everything you felt inside.

Made you question your loyalties.

Made you feel you would never be loved for your true self.

It is my sincerest hope that you have:

Become all you wanted and truly were meant to be.

Have found an abundance of self-love.

Have found the person who is your true love – your fate.

(May you bring each other to cataclysmic orgasm on a regular basis.)

Contents

Epigraph	XI
1. Chapter One	1
2. Chapter Two	17
3. Chapter Three	33
4. Chapter Four	51
5. Chapter Five	69
6. Chapter Six	87
7. Chapter Seven	104
8. Chapter Eight	118
9. Chapter Nine	134
10. Chapter Ten	153
11. Chapter Eleven	169

12.	Chapter Twelve	185
13.	Chapter Thirteen	201
14.	Chapter Fourteen	216
15.	Chapter Fifteen	230
16.	Chapter Sixteen	248
17.	Chapter Seventeen	263
Epilogue		274
About the Author		278
More By Dawn Love		280

"To be yourself in a world that is constantly trying
to make you something else
is the greatest accomplishment."

—— Ralph Waldo Emerson

Chapter One

Arms loaded with a stack of firewood, Jaxon stepped into his mudroom and gently kicked the thick wooden door closed behind him. Pleased that the first significant snowfall of the year had finally arrived, he whistled the melody of one of his favorite songs while he stomped the last of the quickly melting snow from his heavy boots.

As he walked into his cozy living room and placed the load of wood on the storage rack next to the hearth, he spoke to the ball of fur curled into a snuggly circle in front of the roaring fireplace.

"Let's go, Chewy. One more trip into the cold before we call it a night, boy!"

Black ears perked up at the mention of his name, and when Jax called out once more, the dog quickly got up and, with a happy yip, trotted to the back door. At only six months old and already measuring three feet tall at the shoulders, the black and tan Tibetan Mastiff was quickly showing signs of being a giant – gentle, but definitely a giant.

As soon as it was opened, the dog ran out the door, across the back deck, then took a flying leap into the snow. Jax laughed as the rocket of dark fur landed inelegantly in the fluffy piles of white and immediately began to roll, covering himself instantly with tufts of snow.

While the dog happily played and took care of business, Jax looked out across the mountain into the fading light of day and smiled. He loved the mountains, he loved his mountain, and he loved the place he'd built for himself. The small cabin tucked away from everybody and everything was really all he needed.

Two bedrooms – one of which he'd made into his office and command center, a small kitchen, living room, and bathroom. It was a perfect bachelor pad for the hermit life he enjoyed. He was far enough away from town that he didn't often have company, yet he was close enough to still make an appearance a couple of times a week to share a beer with his buddies or to rag on his baby sister.

He shook his head as he thought of her. He could hardly believe that Sera had fallen for one of his best friends. Not because Logan wasn't a great guy, but more that he'd just never seen the signs that there was anything between them more than friendship. Or, he hadn't until things had already progressed to a full-blown relationship. Now, they were planning a wedding, discussing venues and honeymoons - things in which he had absolutely no interest other than being on the periphery.

That's fine, he thought. They could go ahead and get married, start a family – whatever their plans were there - and he would cheer them on. He, on the other hand, was quite happy with things the way they were in his corner of the world. He had his home, his business, and his dog.

He did everything on his own schedule. He worked when he wanted for as long as he wanted. He didn't answer to anyone but himself, and if things continued to go his way, he never would.

He'd spent most of his time during and after college behind a computer screen designing and building programs and applications for various companies around the world. He'd worked his ass off to get noticed, to get the jobs and references he'd needed to succeed. And it hadn't taken long before he made a name for himself as one of the top and most sought-after computer programmers in his field.

Now, he'd done what he'd dreamed of doing for as long as he could remember. He'd started his own company, and the jobs that he once had to chase until he'd built that name for himself, were now falling in his lap, and in some instances, falling and then having to wait in line to be his next undertaking.

He was perfectly content with the path that fate was currently leading him down, and he couldn't imagine life getting much better. He could hole up for hours on end behind his command center and then go for a walk in the woods. He could enjoy the peace and quiet of his little piece of heaven as he downed a cold one by his firepit, or he could drive down the mountain into town and warm a seat at Logan's bar while he listened to the town folk and got the scoop on all the latest.

Quite simply, he could do whatever the hell he wanted, when he wanted, without having to answer to anyone for his decisions.

When the mood struck him, there was usually a woman ready and willing to share her bed – her bed, not his. He always went to them so that he didn't have to deal with the awkwardness of the morning after, using the excuse of his long drive up the mountain to leave as quickly as possible after each encounter.

He never brought anyone home. Never. There was too much of a chance they might want to stay and he didn't want the invasion of his privacy.

As those thoughts floated through his head, a shiver crawled its way through his tall, muscular frame, and a feeling of unease made him look out over the quickly encroaching evening shadows. Though he didn't see anything to be concerned about, he felt that something was off. Suddenly, something just wasn't right.

Knowing that all manner of predators could lurk unseen in the mountains, he quickly whistled for the dog and got them both inside, safe and secure for the night ahead.

Charlotte had absolutely no idea where she was. Well, she thought, that's not entirely true. She knew she was in Colorado, and she knew she was in the mountains. That was something, she supposed.

Though it was only her fourth day of driving, she felt as if she'd been stuck in the car for weeks on end. The last hour of winding through the mountains had tested her patience, her sanity, and her driving abilities.

When the snow had started falling, she'd thought it enchanting and ethereal, but as it had fallen, it had gotten thicker, heavier, and had begun to fall more rapidly than she'd ever seen snow come down. And that, she thought, was saying something as she'd grown up in the often snowy landscape of New England. She'd never had to drive herself in the snow before, almost always depending on the family chauffeur to get her where she was going. She was thankful now that she'd chosen a 4 x 4 from the rental company, but even with the extra traction engaged, she'd quickly begun to slip and slide.

The roads had swiftly become treacherous and now that night had arrived, they'd become even more hazardous. Even slowing to a crawl as she climbed the steep incline, she knew, one wrong move could be deadly.

She'd left her family's estate in northern Vermont with one thing and one thing only on her mind. Escape.

She'd had to get away. Away from her family, away from her responsibilities – away from a life she didn't want and could no longer bear to be a part of. To an outsider, it might seem as if she lived a charmed life, that she had it made, but to her, the world in which she was born was nothing more than a prison.

Yes, she'd been born with a silver spoon in her mouth, but as she'd grown up she'd quickly discovered just how tarnished that spoon had become. Now, unless she did as her family demanded, that spoon and every other item her family owned would be sold off, piece by piece.

If she didn't agree to their demands, they'd face financial ruin, lose everything, and her family would be ostracized from the snotty, upper-class society to which they belonged. These things had been constantly drilled in her head for the past few months and she could no longer take the unbearable pressure she'd been put under by her parents to be the solution to all their financial problems.

She couldn't, wouldn't comply with their wishes and mandates. She'd never cared about the money and had never cared about social standing. All she'd ever wanted was to live in peace on her own terms and without the constant demands of her family and the constraints of upper-class society. Needing time to think and to simply fall off the face of the earth for a while, she'd withdrawn all the cash from her accounts that she could possibly get her hands on, packed a bag with the barest minimum she needed, rented a car, and left that world behind.

She'd snuck out in the middle of the night with no particular destination in mind. She'd known that she'd wanted to go west, and she didn't want to make it easy to be found. When she'd hit I-90, she'd cranked her music and settled in for whatever came her way.

Somewhere outside Albany, New York, she'd bought a burner phone and thrown her personal cell phone in a garbage bin at the entrance to the store. Then she picked up I-84 and slowly began to work her way south and west until she finally reached I-70 in Pittsburgh, Pennsylvania. She'd further covered her tracks by changing out her first rental for the small SUV she now drove, and then she'd gotten back on the road and taken I-70 as a direct shot straight into Grand Junction, Colorado.

It had been a wonderful adventure, so far. She stayed in what her family would have termed "sleezy" motels and ate at mom-and-pop diners. She cringed as she got close to big cities and the traffic increased in volume and speed. Then she celebrated her successful maneuvering as she came out the other side and saw wide-open spaces once again. She marveled at the vastness of the plains and was awe-struck as she gawked at the snow-topped mountains on the distant horizon.

She'd never known just how much of the country she'd missed out on by always flying from destination to destination. She was still uncertain why Colorado had called to her, but it had. And for some reason, she just knew it was going to be the place where she could get lost and stay lost for a very long time.

Well, she thought as she squinted out the windshield and tried to make out her surroundings, she hadn't intended to literally get lost - just to be where her family couldn't locate her. Whatever. So far, it was working.

Her wheels lost traction for the umpteenth time and the back end of the SUV kicked to the side causing her to fishtail and overcorrect as she tried to stay on the road. When the car finally came to a stop, she sat for a moment and caught her breath. Then steeling herself to keep going, she pressed on the accelerator. When the car did nothing but spin its wheels, she groaned and slumped back against the seat in defeat.

She wasn't certain what to do. Should she call for help? Should she stay with the car and hope someone wanders by? Or, should she walk to see if she could find someone to help her?

She pulled out her new phone and opened a map app. Her location appeared, but she was unable to find anything other than a pinpoint that indicated a business named Payne's Programming Solutions. What were the chances, she wondered, that someone would be in the building this late into the evening? She sat for another moment as she debated and calculated the distance. When it dawned on her that it had been more than an hour since she'd last seen a car, she felt the decision was made for her.

Gathering some of her things and bundling into her coat, she exited the car, turned on the flashlight app on her phone, and began walking.

Jax took another pull on his second bottle of beer as he flipped through the satellite channels searching for anything that would hold his interest. When he found a showing of Spaceballs, he grinned and stretched out his long legs, propping his feet on the edge of the sofa. He loved movies from the '80s and '90s and considered himself a pop culture expert.

He'd just begun to quote Dark Helmet's line to Lone Starr declaring their non-relationship when a soft knock sounded on his front door. Jax, unsure he actually heard the knock, muted the television and listened intently. When it came again, he looked to where Chewy soundly slept by the fire and shook his head.

"Good job, dog. Good job."

Grumbling at the interruption and somewhat incredulous that anyone had made the trip up the mountain with the snow coming down so intensely, he flipped on his front porch light and jerked his door open wide. He was fully prepared to give one of his friends all kinds of hell for being out traveling in a snowstorm, but he hadn't been prepared to open the door and find someone he didn't know standing there shivering uncontrollably.

And he most certainly hadn't been prepared to have the woman, clothing encrusted with heavy snow, collapse in his arms. He'd seen her eyes, startled and pleading, begin to roll back in her head as consciousness slowly drained from her body. Instinct and reflexes had him grabbing her before she hit the hard flooring of the porch.

"Well, fuck!" He scooped her limp, lifeless body into his arms and hurried into the house, kicking the door closed behind him and shutting out the bitterly cold winter air. He hurried over to the fireplace and sat with her on the floor. "Fuck, fuck, fuck! Come on, pretty lady. Wake up for me."

He felt the soft skin of her cheek and, finding it ice cold, knew he had to find some way to get her warm. He pulled her backpack and coat off, setting them aside to dry before slipping off her boots and damp socks. Then he reached for the ever-present flannel blanket on his couch and bundled it around both of them, knowing that his body heat and the heat from the fire would warm her much quicker than the blanket alone.

It didn't take long for the chills that wracked her body to begin to subside. Once the shivers passed and her breathing evened out, he carried her to the sofa and tucked the blanket tightly around her.

Throughout it all, Chewy sat and watched, ears perked up, curious but unconcerned with the fact that a stranger had just appeared out of thin air. Just how, Jax wondered, did she get here? He hadn't heard or seen a car, and a quick look out his front door confirmed that he indeed wasn't losing his sight or his hearing.

He looked over to where her backpack sat and found himself sorely tempted to disregard her privacy and go snooping through her belongings. He resisted though, and with another glance at her sleeping form, turned and went to the kitchen to grab yet another beer.

Hopefully, he thought, she would wake up soon and he'd get some answers. But one hour turned into two and before long he gave up and decided to go to bed. He called for Chewy to join him as the dog normally slept at his feet, but when he did, the fluffy ball of fur got up and padded over to the sofa before lying next to it and looking up at Jax with contented eyes.

"Is that the way of it then? Leaving me for a chick? Yeah, yeah. I get it, big guy. He looked to where she lay, beautiful and radiant even in her exhaustion. I definitely get it."

He turned off the television, added a couple more logs to the fire, and went to bed, leaving the dog to keep watch over her as she slept within the gentle glow and warmth of the fireplace.

Charlotte stretched her arms over her head and wiggled her toes, then snuggled back into the plush cushions of the sofa without ever opening her eyes. Waking was and always had been a gradual process for her. She found that no matter how deeply and peacefully she slept, she always wanted just a few more minutes to drift in the luxury of that happy in-between. That sweet spot between sleep and wakefulness was a blissful indulgence she could never seem to resist.

It wasn't until she felt a pair of eyes staring at her that she felt the need to open her own. When she discovered those eyes were big and brown and came with a cold, sniffing nose and lolling tongue, she jerked fully awake and quickly sat up to take in her surroundings.

She had no idea where she was or how she'd gotten there. She remembered the snowstorm. She remembered deciding to walk to find shelter. But much more than that was a blur. She remembered the bitter cold and the steadily falling snow weighing her down the further she went, trudging through the thick drifts as she climbed higher and higher. After that, she only had vague impressions of coming up to the cabin and the relief she felt upon the door starting to open. The rest was a blank.

The yip that greeted her startled her once more and she quickly curled into a ball in the corner of the sofa, uncertain of the friendliness of the four-legged beast whose attention had finally pulled her from her slumber. When the mountain of fluff tilted its head to the side and held up its paw, Charlie smiled and held out her hand for the pup to sniff. Immediately the dog's tail began to happily wag, and her hand was licked in greeting.

"Well, aren't you just a sweet baby!"

"If you call him sweet, I'll never be able to train him as an attack dog."

The deep, gruff voice came from behind her, and she gasped in surprise as she jumped off the couch and turned to see who had made the statement. Her heart thudded in her chest as she looked the man over from head to toe.

Tall and broad of shoulder, his muscular frame filled the doorway he'd just walked through. His dark hair was full and thick on top, fading to a closely shaved buzz cut. A high forehead and strong cheekbones were highlighted by piercing blue eyes that emitted a kindness that instantly put her at ease. A long beard liberally streaked with silver added to the sexy ruggedness of the man before her.

But it was the smile, kind even in its unfamiliarity, he gave her that made her stomach flitter with butterflies and her dusty libido sit up and take notice.

"Sorry. I didn't mean to startle you." He raised a mug of what she assumed was coffee to those fabulous lips and took a sip. "There's coffee in the kitchen if you want. Other than that, your choices are orange juice, beer, and water."

"Uh, coffee would be great. Thanks."

"I'm Jaxon, by the way. You got a name you want to share or am I to keep referring to you as the crazy lady out hiking in a snowstorm?"

"I'm... Charlie. And I wasn't out hiking in a snowstorm. Well, not exactly. My car got stuck. It was either sit and wait and hope that someone found me or take off walking and hope for the best. It's on the side of the road about a mile or so from here. Although, I have to tell you it sure seemed much further than a mile when I was walking."

"A mile in the mountains is quite a bit different than a mile anywhere else. And a mile in the mountains when you're walking through a snowstorm is another thing entirely. Help yourself to the coffee." He nodded his head toward the dog. "I'm going to let Chewy out for a quick run and then we'll see what we can do to get you on your way."

"Thanks. I appreciate it."

She watched as he walked out of the room, calling the dog as he went, and after a few moments, she heard the opening and closing of a door. She took a deep breath and tried to assess her situation. She was alive. She was unharmed. She was lucky, so it seemed, to have found someone who could help. Now what? First things first, she thought and went in search of a bathroom.

Chapter Two

Jax watched as the dog took care of his business and then spent a few minutes rolling and playing in the snow. He'd been awake for the better part of an hour and had already been getting some work done while he'd waited for his unexpected guest to wake.

He'd also been scanning the weather reports and it appeared they were in for another snowfall that afternoon/early evening. By the time that front moved through they would have almost a foot of accumulation. Exactly what he'd been looking forward to, or it had been until he'd found his world invaded by his unexpected guest.

With that much snow forecasted, he wasn't certain how he was going to get her back on the road. Not that he minded looking at her too much. Beautiful. Stunning really. Her hair, waist-length and golden reminded him of Rapunzel, as it had seemed to go on forever. He was fairly certain that was an illusion created by her small stature, and though he considered her short, there was something graceful about the way she carried herself.

Her face had been the kicker for him though. He wasn't certain he'd ever seen so much beauty wrapped up in a face before. Full, plump lips, high cheekbones, and the cutest button nose. But it had been her eyes that had made him shiver. Icy blue and wide with lashes that were so long they brushed her cheeks when she blinked. And the bit that made him drool – no discernable face enhancements. He hadn't seen any trace of makeup across her smooth skin.

The outer package definitely offered a one-two punch that had him catching his breath.

There was something about her that worried him, though. And while he wasn't certain exactly why he felt this way, he couldn't help but think she was hiding something. Hiding and running. It was written in those glacial eyes. Even though his first inclination was to send her on her way, his instincts were telling him to keep her close and protect her at all costs. And didn't that thought just make flutters of panic skitter through his stomach?

Well, he thought as he called to the dog, before he decided whether to listen to those instincts or not, he needed to find out just exactly what story she was selling.

By the time he returned, she'd gotten coffee and had jumped up on a backless stool and made herself at home at the marble-topped island in his kitchen. He glanced in her direction as he hung up his coat and grabbed a towel to rub down the dog. When he'd dried the fur as much as he could, he quickly mopped up the wet and snow they'd tracked into the mudroom and walked into the kitchen to join her.

He refilled his cup then leaned back against his counter, crossed his long legs in front of him, and stared across to where she sat. When she didn't immediately begin telling him how she came to be on his mountain, he realized he was going to have to dig the story out of her.

"So, what is it that you do, Charlie, that makes you feel the need to get away from it all in the middle of a snowstorm?"

"What makes you think that I needed to get away?"

"Well, you're obviously not from this area – I'd know you if you were and there's that New England accent that you cannot hide. Are you just passing through? Visiting friends? Family?"

She grimaced and he knew he'd hit on something. "No. No friends or family. It's beautiful here though, so I'm thinking I might stay for a bit and see how I like it."

"Oh, the mountains are definitely beautiful."

"Can you tell me something?"

"What's that?" Jax questioned.

"Where exactly am I?"

Jax threw his head back as he laughed, full and robust, and she grinned up at him sheepishly.

"That's kind of what I thought. You're not too far, as the crow flies, from Ouray. It's a small town, but it's the closest. Where were you headed?"

"I really didn't have a particular destination in mind. I just wanted to go somewhere in the mountains. How small is this town?"

"Very. It can be a bit touristy in the summer months, but for the most part, everybody knows everybody, or if you don't know them, you know someone who does. Maybe it's a bit cliche, but Ouray may very well be the epitome of small-town USA."

"That sounds just about perfect, actually."

"I suppose. For me? It's just home."

"Well, if you can help me dig out my car and point me in the right direction, I'll get out of your way and go check it out."

"Yeah, that may be easier said than done. I can get you to your car and even dig you out, but if you got stuck last night, I'm going to assume you're not going to be able to handle the extra snow that came down after your arrival. There's about seven inches out there right now, which is about three more than what you hiked up here in. Do you have snow chains?"

"Snow chains?"

"Yes, snow chains. For your tires."

"Umm..."

"Oh, boy. Well, I'm going to assume that if you don't know what they are then you don't have them."

"I'm not certain. I'm in a rental."

"If you got the rental around here then they probably have some in the truck."

"I, uh, didn't get it here." She hesitated, obviously not willing to divulge just where she'd gotten the car, and Jax added her hesitation to a growing list of items that made him feel certain she was on the run.

"Where?"

"I got it just outside of Pittsburgh." Jax rubbed his hand over his face in dismay, a thousand questions blooming in his mind as to who the woman before him was and what was making her skittish.

"Shit."

"Yeah."

"Then it looks like Chewy and I will be trying to drive you down to town. It'll take a while and there's more snow on the way, so we shouldn't wait too long to get going."

"Thank you, Jax. Thank you for everything."

"You're welcome."

―――

The heat from the vents blasted much-needed warmth into the Jeep as Charlie looked out over the rugged landscape of the mountain. Snow had started falling once again, and though she knew that it was adding more treachery to their time on the road, she couldn't help the smile that lit her face as she took in the scenery.

"You know, it was too dark last night for me to truly appreciate what I was seeing. I can't get over how absolutely beautiful it is up here. I bet you take it for granted, seeing it every day."

"You'd be wrong. I never get tired of looking at it. It still makes me feel a certain amount of awe every time I look across the horizon. Yes, I grew up here and it's home, but I've always appreciated just how special it is and how blessed I am to live here."

"Ah, you're an orophile."

"A what?"

"An orophile. Someone who feels peace and serenity in the mountains."

"Umm, okay. I can't say as I've heard that word before, but that sure describes me. I need the mountains. They're vital to my peace and sanity."

Music filled the quiet of the Jeep and the dog perched happily between the front seats so he could look out the windshield. Jax had thrown together a quick breakfast before they left and had even taken the time to show her what snow chains were and how to put them on so she wouldn't be caught unaware again. Then they'd begun their slow descent along the snow-covered path.

"We should be coming to my car soon. I think. Would we be able to stop long enough for me to grab my suitcase out of the back? It looks like I'll be here for a few days while I wait for the opportunity to get back on the road."

"Sure. You said you were about a mile from my house, right?"

"Yes. I think so."

Jax nodded his head to the beat of the music. "It looks like we've got quite a bit of time to kill. Are you going to tell me what brings you to Colorado?"

She'd been afraid he would ask again, and while he was very nice, very welcoming, she certainly didn't want to confide in him, no matter how comfortable she felt in his presence. She had too much at stake to let anyone know who she was and why she was on the run.

"I'm just taking some time for myself and doing some traveling, some sightseeing."

"Uh-huh."

"Uh-huh? That sounds as if you don't believe me."

"That's because I don't."

"That's rude."

"Maybe. But what you don't know because we've just met, is that I'm a damn good judge of character and I'm excellent at reading body language."

"Oh, really?"

"Yes, ma'am."

"And just what do you think you're picking up off of me and my body language, oh insightful one?" Indignation rang throughout her voice and she squared her shoulders and crossed her arms in a huff.

"Alright. I'll give you a rundown of what I know so far. There's New England in your voice, Charlie, and with your statement that you picked up your rental car in Pennsylvania, I know I'm not far off my mark. My ears aren't failing me. You have an air about you – upper class. I can see you at a debutante ball or some other such frivolity. You either don't know to look up at the sky to keep a lookout for bad weather, or you don't know how to read the signs. Otherwise, you wouldn't have even attempted to drive up my mountain yesterday. Going by that upper class that I pointed out, I'm going to say that you've never had to worry about such things, and/or someone else has always done the worrying for you, negating the need for you to learn for yourself. Shall I continue?"

"Oh, by all means – let's hear it!" She rolled her eyes as she turned from looking at him to once again stare out the windshield.

"Alright. Your skin is buffed and polished to perfection and going from the scent of your skin and hair you use high-end products. Not just high-end, but stratosphere level – hundreds of dollars for a few ounces. Fingers and toes? Perfectly manicured and pedicured. The clothes you're wearing are – once again – high-end.

"You're wandering around in the mountains all by yourself. You haven't volunteered your last name, and every time I ask you about what you're doing here, you hedge. In fact, you don't just hedge, you come close to leaping at changing the subject. Not only that but there's some amount of fear in your eyes each time I ask and you're jittery.

"I get the feeling that you're truly a good person who may have just been dealt a bad hand. someone who just needs time to gather her thoughts. Someone who just needs to be on their own for a bit. I don't have a problem with that, Charlie. I don't have a problem with you, or your wanting to run away for whatever reason, but I don't like being lied to or having things hidden from me.

"You don't know me and have no reason to trust me, but I have no reason to out you, no matter who you are and no matter what you're running from."

Silence filled the car as she thought over what he said. He was right on target and she didn't know whether to be ticked that she'd been read so easily or to be pleased that he valued honesty so much. Maybe, she decided, it was a bit of both. She had no idea who he was and had no reason to trust him. So why, she wondered, did she feel as if she could?

At that moment they rounded a curve and found her car. The SUV sat at an angle to the road, somewhat blocking the path down the mountain.

"Whoops."

"Whoops is an understatement. You're lucky nobody came along and plowed into it."

"What should we do, Mountain Man?"

"Mountain Man?" He chuckled as he looked over to where she sat.

"Don't look at me that way. It fits."

Jax looked up at the gray sky through the heat-defrosted windshield and grimaced. "Well, you're probably not going to like this suggestion, but it would probably be best all around if you just went with it."

"Now see, I already don't like the tone in your voice." She huffed out a breath. "Fill me in."

"Well, I hate to tell you this, but if you haven't noticed in all of your astute weather reading, the snow is coming down even harder. I'm not certain we'll make it to town at this rate. My thoughts are that we try to get the rental a bit more out of the way, then we grab your suitcase and go back to my cabin. It's safe. it's warm. And best of all," he grinned cheekily at her, "I have beer."

"But...I..."

"It really is the best option, Charlie. We're about to get piled on. It's going to be a few days before the roads are clear enough to make the trip safely. If you're worried about being alone with me, don't. I'm a good guy. I come with references. Actually, I'm very good friends with a local cop and if you want I can get her on the phone with you right now. She'll vouch for me."

She looked him up and down as she nervously considered, then resigned, reached into her pocket, and pulled out her own phone. She Googled the police department's website and when the number came up, tapped the screen. As the phone started to ring, she put it on speaker and waited.

"Ouray PD. This is Officer Davis. How may I help you?"

"Yes. My name is Charlie and I'm stuck on..." she turned to Jax questioning the name of the road.

"Alex," Jax called out. "It's me. She's got herself stuck in the middle of the road on the way to my cabin."

"Hey, Jax. Yeah, we've gotten a slew of reports of people stuck. The storm hit a little harder than we anticipated. I hate to tell you this, but there's no way we have the extra manpower to come pull her out right now. Your best bet is to hightail it back to your cabin and settle in."

"I figured as much. This is more of a call for you to tell her that I'm a decent guy and that she's safe to stay with me until the roads are passable."

Alex laughed. "Whew! She's lucky it's you and not Ryder. I'll vouch for you any day – Ryder not so much."

"You gotta stop giving him such a hard time, Alex."

"No, I don't. I really don't."

"It was a long time ago."

"Not that long in the grand scheme, Jax. Anyway... Charlie, you have no worries. Jax is a good man and being stuck at his cabin for a few days would not be a hardship. He'll take care of you and you'll get to play with that bear he calls a dog."

Charlie had listened to the back and forth and had already decided she was in good hands. It was obvious that Jax and Alex knew each other well. "And I have the promise of the Ouray Police Department that he won't try to steal my maidenly virtues?" She grinned and blinked her eyes rapidly at him, then tucked her tongue in her cheek as Jax rolled his eyes and Alex began to laugh.

"Steal them? No. Absolutely not. Try to talk you out of them? No guarantees."

"Good enough. Thank you, Alex."

"No problem. Jax, you want me to pass the word along to everyone that you're alive and well?"

"Nah, let 'em wonder. I'll be down in a few days to check in."

"Cool. Gotta go."

Charlie ended the call and sighed. "I guess you're stuck with me."

"And you with me. Let's do this."

By the time they rocked the SUV back and forth and inched it out of the way, the snow had begun to fall so heavily that it was next to impossible to see. They grabbed her suitcase and then made the long trek back to his cabin at a crawl.

Jax carried her suitcase into the house and sat it next to the sofa.

"Unfortunately, I don't have a spare bedroom that's set up as an actual bedroom right now. I use it as my office."

"I'm fine sleeping on the sofa. It's only for a few days."

"Well, you're actually in luck. It's a sleeper sofa."

"Oh, I suppose that works even better."

"Yeah, I upgraded a couple of years ago. After having my buddies get drunk and crash on my couch a few times, I figured it would be a good investment."

"Makes sense." She smiled before she continued. "Thank you for opening your home to me, Jax. I appreciate it."

"It's not much in some people's eyes, but it's perfect for me."

"I can see that."

"Well, make yourself at home. I've got some work I need to do so I'll be holed up in my office for a while."

"Actually, I was going to ask you about that. What kind of work is it that you do? There was a business name that showed on the map last night when I was trying to figure out where I was at."

"I'm an all-around computer geek. I design software."

"That's interesting."

"It can be." Jax stood there for a moment looking awkward. It was as if he was trying to wrap his head around not only having a stranger in his house but also the fact that he was basically leaving her to her own devices while he worked. "If you need something, just knock."

"Alright."

Charlie smiled once again as he walked out of the room. She was grateful for his hospitality even though she could tell it was an effort on his part to extend it. Once the door to his office was closed, she flopped down on the sofa to evaluate exactly what she'd gotten herself into.

In hindsight, she was able to see where she messed up. She definitely should have taken the weather into consideration before leaving Grand Junction the way she had. She just hadn't thought of it. Up until that point, her trip had been very uneventful as far as the weather went so it hadn't even remotely crossed her mind. Well, she thought, now there had definitely been an event and she had something mildly juicy to add to her daily journal. She could see the title of the entry now: Saved by the Mountain Man.

Journaling was new to her but so far she was finding it fun and a nice way to keep track of her new direction in life. She'd only started doing it when she decided to leave home. She hoped that writing down her adventure and her thoughts as she went would help her make sense of her life and the new path it was taking.

She leaned her head back on the sofa, closed her eyes, and relaxed. She grinned when she realized that she was considered missing, on the run, on the lam. What exactly did 'on the lam' refer to, she wondered? One more thing to look up and figure out she supposed.

Her family would never approve of her current situation. Not only that, but they wouldn't approve of the cabin, the man, or the dog. She, on the other hand, was surprisingly pleased and intrigued, and quite comfortable.

She wasn't nervous being there alone with him. In fact, she hadn't felt any trepidation about the situation at all, which she supposed was a good thing. Nice guy. Nice home. She looked toward the hearth where the dog lay napping peacefully. Sweet dog.

Thinking of the tall, muscular man with amazing blue eyes in the room across from her, she let herself begin to drift and was soon fast asleep.

Chapter Three

A sinfully spicy aroma floated in the air and filled her nose as she began to wake up and the familiarity of it made her nostalgic. It also made her hungry and when her stomach gave a loud growl, she came fully awake and propped herself on her elbows to look around in confusion. It only took her a moment to remember her predicament and she cocked her head to the side and listened to see if she could pinpoint the location of her unexpected host. Deciding that the kitchen with its amazing smells was the most likely place, she got up and padded quietly around the corner and into the homey room.

Taking a swig from a bottle of Yeungling, Jax stood in front of the stove stirring a simmering pot of chili. The picture he made as he stood there made her mouth water just as much as the scent of the chili.

"That smells amazing."

Jax turned and looked at her in surprise as he swallowed. "Hey! I didn't hear you come in."

"Sorry."

"It's alright. I'm just not used to having people around. It's a rare occurrence up here."

She narrowed her eyes as she considered. "Which is just the way you like it. You have isolophilia."

"I have what?"

"Isolophilia. You have a strong affection for solitude and being alone."

"Bingo."

"Well, I'll try not to inconvenience you any longer than I have to."

"It's fine. I'm just not..."

"Used to it," she cut him off.

"Yeah. I guess I said that, huh?"

Charlie grinned at him. "So, is that our dinner? Your friend Alex did say you would take care of me and I assume that means feeding me, too."

"Chili is my specialty. You simply can't mess it up."

"I wouldn't know. I don't cook."

"Like, at all?"

"No." Charlie laughed, "I've never learned."

The inquisitive look Jax gave her made her glance away nervously.

"I'm going to assume that you don't care to explain. That's fine. I won't push. It would, however, be nice to know your last name. Wanna share?"

Instinct and ingrained manners had her opening her mouth to answer, but a last-minute realization that she was about to out herself had her stopping in her tracks. She closed her mouth without uttering a sound and dropped her gaze.

Sighing, Jax continued. "That's fine. Just answer a couple of questions to ease my mind, okay?"

"What's that?"

"Did someone physically hurt you?"

"No."

"Is someone going to come looking for you?"

"Maybe."

"Shit. Are you in any kind of danger?"

"No. I promise it isn't like that. Everything is alright. At least for now."

"How long will that last, little rabbit?"

"Little rabbit?"

"Yeah. Rabbit. Because you look like a wary little rabbit whenever you talk, or don't talk, I guess, about yourself, your past, and whoever might be coming for you."

"Oh." She smiled up at him. "Look. They won't hurt me – at least not physically. Mentally and emotionally is another story, but I've sort of been dealing with that most of my life."

"Okay. I think I need to let that sit and simmer in my brain for a bit. I just want you to know that as long as you're with me you're safe."

"Thank you, Jax. I appreciate that."

"This is ready if you are."

"Yes! I'm starving!"

Jax ladled up generous portions into deep bowls and sat them on the island in the kitchen then grabbed another beer from the fridge. "You want a beer?"

"Umm, sure. I've never had one before, but I'm all about new experiences now, so, sure. I'll give it a try."

Stunned, Jax stood with the door to the fridge open and stared at Charlie in disbelief. "Never?"

"Nope. Champagne and an extremely rare occurrence of a mixed drink is the extent of my alcohol knowledge."

"Sheltered. You've lived a very sheltered life, haven't you?"

"Yeah, I guess sheltered just about covers it."

Jax shook his head as he grabbed another beer, popped the tops on both, and sat them next to their bowls of chili. Charlie climbed onto a barstool and spooned up her first bite. Steam rose in swirling tendrils from it and she blew softly across it to cool it off before placing the bite in her mouth. When the savory spices hit her tongue she closed her eyes and moaned.

She slowly chewed as her mind flashed back to the hours she would spend curled up in a nook of their huge kitchen reading a book while the staff prepped and cooked the coming meals. They'd never had chili at their dining table as it was too basic for her family's expensive tastes, but Chef had occasionally had a pot on the stove to feed the staff on those cold winter days. Taking pity on the small, overlooked, and often discarded child she'd been, he'd always shared things with her that he knew she would never experience otherwise. The days that he'd fixed a pot of chili, made her a grilled cheese, or poured her a bowl of Frosted Flakes for a snack, had been some of the most cherished of her childhood memories.

She swallowed and opened her eyes to find him watching her intently. "This is some seriously good chili. It takes me back. Thanks, Jax. For everything."

He'd had a craving for chili while she napped peacefully on his sofa. He'd stood watching her for a few minutes when he emerged from his work cave to begin dinner. He had even taken a photo of her with thoughts of running her through a facial recognition program to figure out just who she was. He'd resisted, though – at least for now. Patience had never been much of a virtue for him and, over the years, he'd had to teach himself repeatedly to slow down and let things happen in their own time. Even now as he stood and watched her eating, his fingers itched to head to his command center and research the woman before him.

He also found himself in the unexpected position of trying to get control of his body. The involuntary reaction he had when she moaned as she tasted the food he'd prepared had brought out some caveman instinct inside him and made some deeply buried need to protect and provide rear its head. It had been all he could do not to straighten his shoulders and stand there preening under her approval. It had been a strange feeling and he now found himself wondering how the hell it had affected him so.

"You're welcome, Little Rabbit."

"Are you seriously going to keep calling me that?"

"Yeah. I think I am. I like it."

When she rolled her eyes at him he couldn't help but smirk. Then spooning up a bite of chili, he dug into his meal. He was halfway through his bowl when she spoke again.

"So, tell me more about this business of yours, Jax. What kind of software do you design."

"Whatever the client needs. I figure out what their end game is and what their needs are. I look at what they have and see if it is something to be improved upon or if it would be easier to start all over. There's a lot of coding and analyzing."

"Oh, that sounds tedious." The lines that appeared between her eyebrows as she pondered his career choice made him want to reach out and smooth them with his thumb. "Resistance is futile," he thought as the Star Trek quote floated through his mind. He could already tell, no longer than this woman had been with him, he was far too invested in her and her origins. She'd certainly occupied his mind most of the afternoon. He just hoped that he would be able to get her out from under his roof before he found himself in over his head.

"Not really. It's what I love to do and I'm damn good at it."

"Oh, that's different then." She smiled up at him as she scooped up another bite. "What is it they say about never really working if you're doing what you love?"

"Yeah, it's something along those lines. I really do love it, though. I love the challenge and I'm a hell of a hacker which comes in handy for designing and setting up all the safety features for the companies I work with."

"It must be nice knowing what you want to do with your life. I'm still figuring that one out."

"What kind of jobs have you done?"

Charlie looked away guiltily. "None."

"Excuse me? None?"

She blew out a breath as she turned back to him, frustration bubbling over as she responded. "Look, you were right on target when you said I was raised in what is considered an upper class of society. I've never worked. I've never had to. I've never done a lot of the things that I'm sure you've done. I've flown all around the world but never driven cross country until now. I've eaten fancy dinners with United Nations ambassadors and heads of state, CEOs of large corporations, and some of the biggest names in Hollywood – millionaires and billionaires, but this is the first time I've sat in a cozy cabin and shared a dinner with a handsome man. Every meal I've ever had has been prepared for me, so no, I've never learned to cook, either.

"I've spent the majority of my life wishing I had been born poor because I have such horrible social anxiety that it makes me physically sick every time I have to shake hands with someone new. I hate going to balls and galas and dinners. Growing up I wished that I had a brother or a sister and could do nothing more than go out and play in a small fenced-in backyard. But no, I didn't get a sibling. I got lessons – swimming, fencing, and ballroom dancing. The list goes on and on.

"I spent my days reading, dreaming, and wishing that I had friends, true friends, and not just acquaintances from boarding school. I've never had girlfriends I could share secrets with, not that I have any secrets worth sharing, but still. I've never gone on an unsupervised date and I've never been intimate with a man. Yes, I've been sheltered and pampered and I hate it. I've hated every minute of it. I just want to be a normal person living a normal life doing normal things. But after twenty-four years it finally occurred to me the only way I was ever going to be able to have any kind of a normal existence was to run away. So, there. Here I am and now you know."

Jax had sat quietly while he'd taken in her tiny tirade. Now he scooped up another bite and chewed thoughtfully before swallowing. "Feel better now?"

Charlie stared at him in disbelief. "Seriously? I lay all that at your feet and all you have to say or ask is if I feel better now?"

"Yep."

"I don't even... I can't... How can you sit there so calmly after I went off like that?"

"Because you obviously needed to let it out. Venting is natural. It's needed. Everyone deserves the opportunity to go on a rant and clear out what they've bottled up. Although, as you've dealt with this your entire life, I suspect you could use a few more sessions."

She couldn't help the bewilderment she felt. "Who are you? A saint? You take me into your home when I pass out on your doorstep. You didn't take advantage of me when I was passed out. You offered to share your home with me for a few days, cook me the best damn meal I've had in years, and then you let me lose my stuff on you. I'm baffled."

"Lose your 'stuff'?" Jax laughed loudly. "Little Rabbit, if you're serious about living in the real world and getting some real-world experience, then I'm going to need you to know that it's alright to cuss. In fact, I highly recommend it. Say it with me, okay? Shit. The word you're looking for is shit."

Charlie grinned at him. "Shit."

"See?" He smiled back at her in amusement, "That works so much better. You lost your shit and it's okay."

"I lost my shit and it's okay." She thought about it for a moment. "I like it. I lost my shit and I'm drinking beer and eating chili."

"Well, technically, you haven't taken a drink of your beer yet."

"Oh! Yeah. Okay. Here I go." Charlie picked up the bottle and turned it in her hand as she studied the label. "Alright. I'm going to do it. I'm going to drink beer." She turned up the bottle and took a large gulp then made a face as she swallowed. Jax laughed loudly, the sound reverberating off the walls of the cabin.

"Well, should I take the look on your face as any indication of what you think about it? Because going by that I would say that maybe beer isn't your drink."

"No. I just think I need to get accustomed to it. I'm reserving my verdict until I've had more of it. I'm no quitter – well if you don't include the whole quitting my life and starting over thing, that is. That doesn't count, does it?"

He shook his head, "No. We won't count that. This is your new life and in this life, you're definitely no quitter."

She laid her hand on his forearm and looked deeply into his eyes. "Seriously, Jax. Thank you."

"You're welcome, Charlie. By the way, you're on dish duty."

"Fair enough."

Jax sank into the sofa and stretched his long legs out in front of him as he reached for the TV remote and began flipping through channels. After they finished their dinner, he took the dog out for bladder relief and watched as the snow continued to pile up. They were easily at twelve inches and it was still coming down. Funny, he thought, the idea of being stuck in the cabin with his unexpected guest wasn't irking him as much as he thought it would. He found her interesting, a bit lost, extremely inexperienced, but definitely interesting and he found he wanted to know more about her. Yeah, he thought, like a fucking last name. That would be great.

He was still resisting the urge to use his facial recognition software, but if she didn't tell him soon, he was going to give in. He really didn't want to invade her privacy like that, but part of him desperately wanted to know what kind of potential trouble might land on his doorstep. His initial thought had been romantic trouble with a spouse or boyfriend/girlfriend, but after her tirade at dinner, he now doubted that and had started leaning more toward a familial problem. The itch to hunker down behind his computer and hack his way into her life began to make him twitch.

He was about to give in when he flipped past a news channel and a brief glimpse of a missing person's photo stopped him in his tracks. He quickly flipped back for a better look. When he realized that the icy blue eyes and long blond hair of the person in the picture belonged to the woman currently in his kitchen washing dishes for the first time in her life, dread settled in the pit of his stomach like a lead balloon. He turned up the volume so that he could hear what the news anchor was saying.

"...Ms. Abbingdon was last seen a week ago at her family's Vermont estate. Her parents are understandably worried for her safety. Police are still investigating but at this time no evidence of foul play is suspected. If you have any information as to the whereabouts of Charlotte Grace Abbingdon, please contact the Vermont State Police immediately."

Before the graphic disappeared, he quickly paused the livestream and sat upright staring at the image before him. Well, he thought, that answered at least one question. Now that he knew her name he was uncertain how he wanted to handle things. Should he tell her? Should he keep quiet and do some digging? Should he wait patiently for her to open up? He was sitting and scratching his head over it when he heard her coming. Fumbling the remote in his haste, he unpaused the newscast and changed channels. As she rounded the corner, he looked up at her and hoped like hell he was hiding the guilty look he was certain was showing on his face.

"Dishes are officially done!"

Jax grinned, "And how was your first experience with manual labor?"

Charlie curled up on the sofa, tucking her feet beneath her as she got comfortable. "I like it. It made me feel useful and that is something that I've never felt before."

"Well then, by all means, let's help you to feel useful. How about, for the remainder of your stay, you take dish duty? I've never minded cooking but doing the dishes afterward has always been a pain in my ass."

"I can do that. In fact, if there's anything else around here I can help with, just let me know. You may have to give me instructions, but I'm more than willing to learn and be helpful."

"Alright. We'll see what comes along."

"So what are you watching?"

He looked back at the television as if it were a foreign object. "Oh. I haven't found anything yet. What would you like to look at?"

"I don't suppose I care. I don't normally watch much TV."

Jax grabbed his chest in mock horror. "How do you survive?"

"I read. I read all the time. Books are one of the greatest joys of my life!"

"Well, that's cool. I enjoy reading, too, but when I want to just zone out for a while, television and movies are it for me. What kind of books do you read?"

"Oh, I read a bit of everything. I love mystery, horror, and romance. True crime is pretty interesting to me, too, but lately, I've been on a romance kick."

"Alright. Favorite author?"

"Wow! There are so many! There is this newer author I've been reading and I devour everything she publishes. Her name is Seraphina Devine and she is absolutely fabulous! I follow everything she does and stalk her social media. I simply can't get enough of her and her writing!"

Jax shook his head in disbelief. "I suppose I shouldn't be surprised." Standing, he held out his hand to her. "Come with me."

Confused, Charlie hesitated before she placed her hand in his and followed behind as he pulled her into his office. Once inside, he dropped her hand and with both arms opened wide, gestured at a bookshelf that ran the length of the wall.

"Oh! Oh my gosh! You're a Seraphina Devine fan!"

"Yes and no."

"What do you mean, yes and no? You have all of her books so you must be a fan!"

"Yes, I'm a fan. However, I have not read any of these books."

"Well, that just makes no sense whatsoever!"

"I love Seraphina Devine with all my heart. I will purchase every book she writes, but I can never read them. At least, I'll never read them as long as the books she publishes have sexual content in them."

"I'm so confused. Explain."

"Sera is my sister."

"What? Seriously?" Excitement rang out in her voice. "That's fantastic! Oh! Oh! I see! No, I suppose you wouldn't want to read some of the things she writes. She is very detailed and writes extremely intimate scenes. I can understand how that would make you uncomfortable."

"Yeah, I don't need that much of a glimpse into my sister's mind. And now that she's with Logan, one of those friends who used to invade my sofa after too many drinks, I just have this sinking suspicion that things are even more graphic." He shook his head in denial. "Nope. I can't even begin to read one of those."

She reached for one of the books and took it from the shelf. "Oh! This one was quite possibly my absolute favorite of hers. It was so romantic and exciting." Her cheeks suddenly changed color, a rosy blush blooming across them. "And graphic. Very, very graphic."

"Yeah, see... You can stop right there. This is the one she wrote while she and Logan were getting together. Nope. I don't want or need to know anything about what's in that book."

She smiled up at him as she replaced the book on the shelf and the innocence in the look she gave him stirred something deep inside him. "Thank you for sharing this with me, Jax. Maybe one of these days I'll get to meet her."

"If you're planning on staying in Ouray for very long you'll get to meet her. She and Logan live above his bar."

"That would be amazing!"

She turned then and walked back into the living room. Jax watched her walk out and as he did, he couldn't help but notice she looked just as good going as she did coming. Well, hell, he thought as he ran a hand through his thick hair and contemplated his next move. Should he come clean with her? Should he tell her he knew who she was? Should he do some more digging? Should he help her hide? Should he pick her up, kiss the hell out of her, and get a taste of those ripe lips? The possibilities were endless.

And then something she'd said earlier in the evening broke through his memory and made his body come to attention. Holy shit, he thought, she's a virgin! He ran a hand down his face and moaned silently as more of those possibilities started playing on a loop through his brain and he softly whispered one long, drawn-out word.

"Fuck..."

Chapter Four

The next morning Charlie woke to the feel of hot breath on her face and the press of a cold nose to her cheek. Confused, she startled awake and found herself staring into Chewy's curious eyes.

"Oh! It's you!" She laughed as she reached for the dog and began to ruffle his thick fur. "Good morning, Chewy!" The dog immediately climbed on top of her and began licking her face. She giggled as he showed her just how happy he was to receive her attention.

"Alright, alright. I'm up." She sat up and looked around the living room. "Where's Jax? Huh? Where's he at, boy?"

She climbed out of bed and stretched as she walked into the kitchen, the aroma of freshly brewed coffee calling her. She filled a mug and took a sip, enjoying the shock of caffeine as it hit her system. When she still saw no signs of Jax, she decided to hit the shower, assuming he had probably been up for a while and was already holed up behind his workstation. She quietly padded down the hallway and opened the bathroom door.

What she saw when she opened the door made her stop in her tracks, and the coffee cup began to slip from her hand. Jax had just stepped out of the shower and stood on a bathmat completely naked rubbing a towel over his muscular, wet body. His head turned to her in surprise and seeing the cup slowly slipping from her grip, he reached out and caught it before it fell to the floor, somehow miraculously keeping it from spilling a single drop.

"Whoa..."

"Oh, my God. Oh, my God. I'm sorry. I'm so sorry. I...I didn't know you were in here." She couldn't stop staring even as she apologized. A string of thoughts ran rapidly through her mind as she took in the beautiful specimen who stood before her in all his God-given glory. He's naked. He's wet and naked. He's...wow. He's magnificent.

She was speechless as she continued to look him up and down from head to toe. She wasn't completely naive. She'd seen photos of naked men before. She'd visited numerous museums and galleries where there were marble statues of naked men, and paintings with every detail of the male specimen highlighted. But, holy schnitzel, she thought, she'd never seen a naked man up close and personal before. She was completely entranced as she stood there. Entranced, and instantly turned on.

Jax sat the coffee mug on the bathroom sink, an amused expression splitting his face into a wide grin, as he then took his time wrapping the towel around his waist.

"Good morning, Little Rabbit. Is there something I can help you with?"

"I, uh, I was just going to take a shower. But you're here. Umm, I can wait. I should...I should go and leave you to it." She couldn't take her eyes off his chest, or at least she couldn't now that other parts of him were covered. "So, I'll, uh, yeah..."

She turned to leave and had just stepped outside the bathroom when he stopped her.

"Charlie?" She stopped where she was but didn't look back. "You might want your coffee."

"Oh, yeah. I almost forgot." She turned then and was once again met with a broad, muscular chest. Timidly, she grabbed the coffee and backed out of the room, closing the door as she went.

In a daze, she walked down the hall and back to the kitchen. She climbed on one of the stools at the long island countertop and all but melted into the seat. Images of Jax completely naked, his skin rosy from the heat of his shower, water droplets still clinging to his skin, floated through her brain leaving her feeling things she'd never felt before. She had been attracted to men before, but not like this. No, she thought, certainly not like this.

She had thought he was good-looking, but now that she'd seen him without a stitch of clothing on she knew, he wasn't just good-looking, he was a masterpiece. A sexy, mouth-watering masterpiece.

Jax stood there grinning long after she left the bathroom. He couldn't help but go back over the scene in his head once more. The look on her face had been priceless, and the fact that seeing him naked had caused her to ramble, made him want to preen like a peacock. He turned to the mirror and gave his physique a once over. He had a gym membership but he didn't use it as often as he should. Most of the time he got his workouts in by doing things like hiking and chopping wood. He supposed the combination was working for him.

He'd always been more muscular than his friends – he was just built bigger than they were. He supposed burly would be a good word to describe himself. His friends liked to tease him that he was the epitome of a mountain man.

Jackasses.

Whatever. They could tease all they wanted. They were the ones who spent their lives in the gym lifting weights and trying to catch up to him.

Charlie's flushed cheeks flashed through his mind once more. He still couldn't seem to wrap his mind around the fact that she was a virgin. How on earth had she not already been snatched up by some Harvard dude with loads of family money?

They'd stayed up late the night before watching movies so he hadn't had time to go digging into her background. His fingers were itching for his keyboard. But, first things first, he thought as his stomach growled. He pulled on a pair of gray sweatpants and a white T-shirt, then headed for the kitchen.

When he rounded the corner, he stopped in his tracks. She sat at his kitchen counter with a dreamy look on her face. He suddenly found himself hoping that dreamy look was caused by their bathroom encounter. Then another thought hit him like a ton of bricks. Seeing her sitting in his kitchen drinking a cup of coffee? She just looked... right. It was as if that was where she belonged.

The thought zinged through his head like a metal ball in a pinball machine and made him panic. All he could think at that point was, oh hell no...

He shook his head to clear out the unwanted thoughts and continued into the kitchen. When she saw him, she straightened in her seat and cleared her throat before taking another sip of coffee. Jax reached for a mug and filled it before turning to look at her.

"Hungry?"

She nodded her head. "Yes, actually I am."

"Go ahead and get your shower. I'll have breakfast ready when you get out."

She smiled at him as she slid off the stool and started through the doorway. Then she stopped and turned to face him, "Jax?"

"Yeah?"

"Thank you."

"For what?"

"For everything. You're giving me shelter and food out of necessity, but you allowed me to unload on you last night, and just now, well, you could have given me a hard time about walking in on you and instead you're allowing me to have my dignity. So, thank you."

Stunned, he didn't know quite what to say, but he didn't get the chance to say anything at all as she turned and left him standing there. Well, hell, he thought. She thinks I'm this good guy when in truth all I can think about is taking her to bed and showing her just what she's been missing.

Fuck.

Charlie had a thing for long, hot showers. Unfortunately, Jaxon's water heater didn't allow for such luxuries. She felt as if she'd just barely started going through her routine when the water temperature had begun to slowly fade from boiling to iceberg cold. As soon as she realized what was happening she began to hurry in hopes that she would be done before she turned to a popsicle. It was a race she did not win.

She quickly stepped from the shower and wrapped herself in a fluffy towel to try to warm up for a moment before she began to dry off. Though it helped, she couldn't seem to stop the shivers that had started wracking her body the moment the hot water disappeared. She dried off as best she could and then wrapped the towel around her once more, and still her body shook from the frigid water temperature.

After a moment she decided the best thing she could do would be to just get dressed. Then it hit her. She had been so stunned and wound up from walking in on Jax naked that she'd forgotten to grab any clean clothes to put on after her shower. Fiddlesticks, she thought! She grabbed an extra towel, wrapped up her long hair, and then eased the bathroom door open. Looking left and then right she made sure the path was clear and then tiptoed down the hallway to the living room.

The warmth radiating from the roaring fire in the fireplace distracted her and she took a moment to stand in front of it to ease the chill from her icy shower. She warmed her front, then her back, then turned once more to face the fire. She closed her eyes and basked for a moment more and then Jax's deep voice filled the room and startled her.

"Well, now, that's a sight."

She jumped and let out a high-pitched squeal as she turned to see him lounging against the doorframe. When she did, the hold she had on the towel she'd wrapped around her body slipped and it began to fall. She fumbled for the soft cloth and quickly tried to cover her nakedness. As she stood there with the material clutched tightly against her body, she stared at Jax in shock.

"Oh my God! You scared the daylights out of me!"

"I would say I'm sorry, but I'm rather enjoying the view." He grinned at her, amusement dripping throughout his voice as he continued to lean against the frame, arms crossed and looking her body over from head to toe.

"I, uh, forgot to take my clothes with me. I guess my mind was elsewhere."

"Freudian slip?" The mischievous glint sparkling in his baby blues ruffled her feathers and she narrowed her eyes at him.

"Not funny. Not in the least."

Jax laughed, full and robust, before he continued. "I'm just messing with you. I wanted to let you know breakfast is ready. Go ahead and get dressed, but... you're welcome to come as you are. I'll be in the kitchen." With that, he turned and left her standing there, astonished at his audacity.

Once he was out of sight, she re-wrapped the towel around her body and went in search of her clothes, mumbling as she went.

"Freudian slip. Freudian slip, my butt. Wait. That should be ass, not butt. Freudian slip, my ass! Oh! He's right! That is so much better!"

"So, tell me about growing up privileged." Jax popped a piece of bacon in his mouth and chewed while he waited for her answer. He'd been pleasantly surprised to find her standing in front of his fireplace wrapped in nothing but a towel. Sexy, he thought. She's so damn sexy. Even better, she has no idea she's sexy which makes her even sexier. He had always been drawn to women who had no idea of just how appealing they were. Intelligent. So far, everything she said pointed to high intelligence, even savant level in some instances. A pretty face could draw him, and a sexy body would make him lust, but intelligence had always been a huge turn-on for him. Humor. Humor went a long way with him, too. Once again he asked himself just how it was that nobody had snatched her up and held on tight.

"What do you want to know?"

"Everything. What was it like growing up and never having to worry about money?" There had been times when his mother had no choice but to scrimp and save. After his dad had died things had been tight. They had managed, but it wasn't until his mom had met Sera's dad that financial constraints had eased for them.

"That's just it. I never had to think about it. It was always just there. Things I needed were always just there. Did I take things for granted? Absolutely. Even in boarding school I never wanted for anything. Well, except companionship. I was so sheltered growing up that I had no idea how to make friends. The one thing I wanted and needed more than anything and I had no idea how to make it happen. I spent four years in Switzerland, was only visited by my family on rare occasions, and the entire time I was there I hid away in my room. The other girls at the school were nice to me, but they were ambivalent about my existence. I was there, but I wasn't a part of things. I wasn't in any of the friend groups. Yes, they would say hi and speak to me when I walked by, but they never missed me when I wasn't around."

"When you weren't in class or studying, what did you do with yourself? What occupied your free time?"

"I read. In fact, I read all the time. On the rare occasion I wasn't reading, I was researching on my own, learning about things I was interested in the school didn't teach."

"And when you were home? What was that like?"

"Not much different, actually. I didn't have friends there, either. I had a nanny growing up and rarely saw my parents. I was brought out and paraded in front of their friends and guests when they did acknowledge my existence. That was only to show me off, though. Look at our beautiful, intelligent daughter. She'll make a fine wife for one of your sons someday. I suppose my nanny was the closest thing I had to a friend, and that's a stretch. She would play with me but it never seemed it was just for fun. There was always a lesson behind everything she did. Between school and all my various other lessons, I didn't have that much free time, but when I did I would sneak down to the kitchen. You see, the staff was always kinder to me than my parents.

"There is a large bay window in the kitchen that looks out on the grounds. I always took a book with me and curled up on the seat. I loved having the noise of the kitchen around me, the heat from the stoves and ovens, the hustle and bustle as the staff worked to make things perfect. Our house always seemed so cold, not just temperature-wise, but the atmosphere. Not the kitchen. It always radiated warmth – physical warmth and emotional warmth. Our staff was always welcoming and inviting. Cook always took care of me. He always made sure I got to try things and taste foods that would never be served at my parents' table. The kitchen and the people in it were my querencia, my safe place, the place I felt most at home."

"How do you do that?"

"What?"

"How do you just pull random odd words or words from another language from thin air? You've done that several times since you've been here."

"I love languages. I love words. I'm a linguaphile. All those years in boarding school when I was studying on my own? I was studying languages, learning odd or unusual words, words that have been slowly forgotten from our everyday lexicon."

"And you can just pull these words out randomly? Do you even have to think about them, or are they just there?"

"No. I don't have to think about them. Once I learn a word it stays with me. I pepper them throughout my sentences without even thinking about it."

"You pepper unusual words and other languages, and I pepper curse words." Jaxon laughed and then drank down the remainder of his coffee.

"What about you, Jax? What was your world like when you were growing up?"

He stood and took his dishes to the sink. "Different. It was far different than your world. I'll have to tell you about it another time, though. I've got to get some work done."

"Alright. I'll clean up the dishes and find something to occupy me. Don't let me keep you from your business."

"Sounds good."

With that, Jax left her sitting in his kitchen. He truly did have work to do, but once he had some of that out of the way he intended to do the digging he'd been wanting to do ever since she'd fainted in his arms.

Photos. There were photos of her with her hair perfectly coiffed, makeup expertly applied, wearing expensive dresses and flowing gowns. He lost count of the number of events she had attended and the photographs that had been taken. She had gone to these functions and though there were large groups of people in each photo, she somehow always managed to appear separate from the throng – there, but not a part of the clique. It was as if she were nothing more than window dressing. The only common denominator he could find in all of them was the look of loneliness that lurked beneath the facade she wore like a second skin. How, he wondered, could she look as if she belonged yet didn't belong, simultaneously?

He found page after page of information on her family, their holdings, and their inherited wealth. That didn't hold much interest for him, though and he only did a cursory dig on the financials. Although she made appearances in photo after photo, the true nitty gritty he had been hoping to find simply was not readily there. It was as she said – her family paraded her around for show but when it came time to do more than present an image, she was left out, tossed aside, and her parents' personal agenda pushed to the forefront.

It had just been over forty-eight hours since she stumbled into his life and he already felt he knew her better than her parents ever would.

He continued to search, unearthing photos of her as a young child, and photos of her as a teen. The articles on her family, their social standing, and their wealth never failed to mention her but it was always an afterthought and brief in content. From all he found and the few conversations they'd had so far, he quickly formed the opinion that her parents had brought her into the world as an obligation, a duty filled to carry on their legacy, and not out of love or true want for a child.

It was foreign to him and he didn't know if he could ever understand people like that. His home had always been filled with love and laughter, a sense of being wanted and cherished. When his father passed, he, his mother, and his older sister grew closer than ever. Then when his mother remarried and brought his stepfather and Sera into his life, that love had grown and expanded.

Then there were his two best friends. Ryder and Logan had always been there for him, just as he had been for them. They had been inseparable and that remained unchanged even though they were now adults with careers and responsibilities.

A family who treated her as a commodity, with no friends to play with, to confide in - he couldn't imagine the isolated loneliness Charlie had obviously felt her entire life.

Jax stretched and looked at the time. As usual, he had lost track of just how long he had been behind his command center. He called for Chewy so he could take him out for a run, but his furry friend didn't appear. Curious, he went to investigate. After looking for him in all his usual spots and not finding him, he went to look out the back windows. What he saw brought a smile to his face.

Charlie, bundled head to toe against the cold, picked up Chewy's well-loved tennis ball and gave it a throw. The dog, deliriously happy, ran after his prey, dug it out of the snow, and returned it to her to be thrown once more. They made quite a sight and Jax couldn't keep the smile from his face. After several throws, Chewy's excitement grew. Jax saw it coming but wasn't quick enough to warn Charlie. The dog scooped up the ball and came bounding back to her. This time, though, he didn't stop. Taking a flying leap, Chewy tackled her and sent them both tumbling to the ground.

Jax was out the door and running to her as quickly as he could through the deep snow. By the time he reached them, Chewy was lying on top of her licking her face, deliriously happy with his new friend.

"Chewy! Off!" With sad eyes, the dog looked up at him and reluctantly took off running through the snow once more. "Charlie! Are you alright?" She lay in the snow staring up at the sky, giggling and gasping for breath.

"Yes. I, I think so."

Jax held out a hand to help her up. "Come on. Let's get you inside."

"I don't think I can move yet. I'm still trying to catch my breath."

"Well, you can't just keep laying there in the snow." He reached for her then and simply scooped her up into his arms. "I've got you."

He hurried inside and called for the dog as they went. Once they were in the toasty warmth of his home, he sat her on top of the washing machine in the mudroom and began to help her out of the heavy layers she wore.

"I can do this, Jax. Just give me a minute."

"I'm sure you can, but it's the least I can do after my bumbling dog tried to take you out."

She laughed then and the bell tone sent shivers of need coursing through him. He briefly closed his eyes to try to tamp down that need and then reached for her boots. Once they were off and sitting on a mat to dry, he stepped back to her and with his hands on her waist, lifted her off the machine and onto her feet. A sensual flash of taking her on the washing machine ran through his mind and made him take a quick step back in retreat.

"Thanks for taking Chewy out. I'm sorry he has no manners. I promise we've been working on it."

"I'm okay and I enjoyed taking him out. Well, until he decided to use me as a sofa, that is." Once again she laughed. "I think I'm going to go warm up by the fire for a bit."

She turned then and left him standing there wondering what the hell was wrong with him that he couldn't seem to control his thoughts around her. Damn it, he thought, this isn't good. Not at all.

Chapter Five

Charlie tucked her feet beneath her and covered herself with a blanket as she got comfortable on the sofa in front of the fireplace. She reached for her current read and was two chapters in when Jax entered the living room with a cup filled with steaming liquid held out to her.

"Here. Hot cocoa. It'll help warm you up."

"Thank you, but you really didn't have to do that."

"I know. But it's one of the things I love after being out in the snow."

Jax lifted a mug of his own and took a sip as he sat on the opposite end of the sofa and turned to her.

"What?"

"Okay, I have a couple of things to tell you. First, believe it or not, it has warmed up some out there. The sun has been out all day and if it continues to warm up, we may be able to get you to town tomorrow."

"Oh! That would be great! I appreciate your hospitality – grudging that it is – but I should really try to find a place in Ouray and get myself out of your hair."

"I still don't think we need to try to get your car down there, but I should be able to make it in my Jeep without any trouble if it melts a bit more. I'll get you there."

"Thank you, Jax."

"Don't thank me yet." The tone of his voice changed and instantly made the hair on the back of her neck stand at attention. "I have a confession."

She could do nothing but stare at him. She was certain she knew what he was going to say and panic began to rise in her chest.

"I know who you are, Charlie."

"What are you talking about?"

"I know, Charlotte. I've known since last night after dinner. I was flipping through the channels on the TV and ran across a news report. You're a wanted woman."

She set her mug on the small table next to the sofa and immediately rose to begin pacing. Back and forth she went, chewing a thumbnail in contemplation. Then she stopped in front of him and stared with a pleading look.

"I can pay you."

"What?"

"I can pay you."

"Wait. What the hell are you talking about?"

"I will pay you to keep quiet. I know there's a reward. I will pay you double what they're offering if you'll keep my secret."

"Whoa... Hold up right there. First, I have no intention of turning you in. Second, I don't need nor want your money. Third, just what kind of person do you think I am that I would do that to you?"

Taken aback, all she could do was stare at him.

"You confided in me what your old life was like, what you've lived with. I would never betray that kind of confidence. I know you don't know me well or really at all, but I'm not built that way. I would never, could never do that to you."

Panic that had been fluttering in her chest began to ease and her shoulders slowly relaxed.

"Thank you, Jaxon. You can't possibly know what it means to me to hear that. I don't want to go back. I just can't. I don't think I can ever go back to living my life that way. I wasn't living. I was existing and I was miserable."

"Then you won't go back. This is your new life and it can be whatever you want it to be." The smile on his face was kind and understanding.

"I'm not certain what that is yet, but I'm determined and excited to find out."

"Well, not that my opinion matters much, but Ouray is a great place to settle down and figure out life."

At ease once more, she curled back up on the sofa and took a sip of her cocoa. "If nothing else, I think it's a great starting point. I can't wait to see the town."

"This brings about the third thing I wanted to talk to you about. My sister has an apartment that is unrented at the moment. I spoke with her while I was making the cocoa and she confirmed that not only is it unoccupied, it is partially furnished. When she moved in with Logan they combined their belongings but there was quite a bit they decided they didn't need. Part of her stuff got moved into his place; part of his stuff got moved into hers. If after you take a look at the town you decide to stay, the apartment is yours if you want it."

"Are you serious?"

"Absolutely."

"That would be amazing!"

"Then tomorrow, we'll get you to town, take you on a tour, let you meet my friends and my sister, and then you can make a decision. I don't think you'll be sorry."

"Oh, my God! I'm going to meet Seraphina Devine! I'm giddy!"

Jax laughed. "I told her about you and you being a fan and she is excited to meet you."

"She...she knows?" She couldn't keep the dismay out of her voice.

"What? Oh! No! No, Charlie. I didn't tell her about your true identity. If after you meet her you feel the need to share, you won't have to worry about her telling anyone or selling you out. She may be my step-sister but we're cut from the same cloth. I promise you if you tell her, she will keep your secret."

"Whew. Okay. Okay. Thank you. Thank you for everything, Jax."

"Anytime."

The next day Jax made a right-hand turn and drove south on the highway, then straight into Ouray. It had been a long, slow drive, but his Jeep had handled the snow-covered road like a champ. Unsure of what kind of road conditions they would find and how long it might take them to get there, Jax had loaded essentials for him and Chewy into the Jeep. If the roads were too bad or if the weather took a turn, he would just crash at Ryder's for the night.

He enjoyed the conversation they shared on the way into town. But it had been the awe on her face and the excitement in her voice that made the trip memorable for him. The roads in town had been cleared well and he drove her from one end to the other and back again, looping through a few side streets to point out different things of interest. She immediately wanted to explore, but he was able to convince her that meeting up with Sera and Logan should be first on the agenda.

Introducing Charlie to Sera had been quite entertaining. Charlie's porcelain complexion turned a beautiful shade of pink as she gushed and blushed while shaking hands. Jax found it quite endearing. She blushed almost as much when she shook hands with Logan. He assumed she was remembering some passage from Sera's book and he found it amusing but uncomfortable at the same time. He wasn't sure how he felt about Charlie knowing intimate details of Logan and Sera's relationship. He knew Sera changed the names in the book, but most of the story was theirs right down the line – or so Sera had said.

Now, they sat in Logan and Sera's living room discussing the apartment, with Charlie and Sera speaking as if they were old friends. This, he thought, may work out to be a wonderful friendship for her.

"Ladies," said Logan, "can I interest you in some coffee?" Logan ran a hand over his tired face as he looked back and forth between them.

"Long night?" Jax knew it was much earlier than Logan liked to be up. Running his bar often kept him up late into the night and sleeping while the rest of the world went about their business.

"Two fights – one of which was between my damn waitresses. It took a while to get the cleanup done and to sort things out between the girls. I'm afraid I'm going to have to let Heather go. She's been causing problems for a while now."

Sera looked at her fiance and rolled her eyes. "That girl has been making trouble ever since you turned her down last year."

"Yeah, well, she didn't take it too well."

"That's an understatement."

"What can I say? I only have eyes for you." Logan smiled at Sera. "Alright, coffee will be ready in just a minute. Why don't you join me, Jax?"

"Huh? What?" Jax had been lost in his own little world for a moment imagining what a night out with Charlie might bring. He had a feeling she had probably never set foot in an actual bar before.

"Coffee. Kitchen. You. Me. Now."

Jax rolled his eyes and got up to join him. When he stepped into the kitchen Logan was loading the coffee into the filter.

"Why exactly did I need to help you make coffee?"

"You know damn good and well this has nothing to do with coffee. Spill."

"Spill what?" Jax looked at his friend curiously.

"Don't be dense, asshole. Your body is but your brain isn't."

"Jealous that I don't have to work out to maintain this physique, aren't ya?"

"Whatever. Like I said, spill." Logan grabbed a tray and began loading it with mugs, creamer, and sugar.

"There isn't much to spill, Logan. She got lost in the storm the other night and ended up on my doorstep. She's been with me ever since. She needs a place to stay for a bit and you and Sera have an available apartment. End of story."

"Bullshit. There's more. I know there's more because I know how to read people. She's hiding something or from something, and you're being very closed-mouthed about whatever it is. Luckily, I've got Sera and she is a master at digging out details. She also can't keep a secret from me to save her life."

"Look. Charlie has some...stuff...to deal with. She's starting a new life. If she decides to tell Sera or you or pop onto the web and make an announcement to the world, that's her business. It isn't my story to tell."

"Alright. I get it. Just tell me this, and I'm only asking because I have Sera to look out for, is she in trouble?"

Jax blew out a breath. "I don't know man. She says she isn't, but I feel like she didn't give me the full story. I can see the potential for issues. I just don't know what they are or from where they might come."

"Shit."

"Yeah. Shit. I will promise you this, if she tells me there is something to be worried about, I will let you know. Sera may be yours now, but she is and will always be my little sister."

"Fair enough. Grab that pot and bring it with you. I need some caffeine if I'm going to deal with bookish talk this early in the damn morning.

Jax chuckled at his friend, but grabbed the pot full of coffee and re-joined the small gathering in the living room.

Charlie sat facing Sera on the sofa, a look of bewilderment on her face. "Goodness! I still can't believe I'm sitting here talking with you. I never dreamed I would ever get the opportunity to meet you in person."

Sera laughed. "Well, I'm not sure what hand of fate brought you our way, but I'm glad it did. I love interacting with my fans, but I rarely get the opportunity to meet them in person. It'll be nice having someone else around to talk books with. Jax can't seem to bring himself to discuss things with me." She looked at her brother and rolled her eyes, "My friend, Alex, loves to read my books but she reads them, loves them, and almost instantly forgets what was in them. It's nice to have some feedback from someone who retains the stories. While I love talking books with Logan, he much prefers for me to experiment on him with the scenes I write – you know, just to make sure everything works as it should."

Charlie's face flamed beet red and Sera doubled over with laughter.

"Really, Sera?" Jax and Logan spoke simultaneously.

"Sorry! I had to. Gosh, the looks on each of your faces. Priceless. Absolutely priceless."

"Can we get back to setting Charlie up with the apartment? If I'm going to make it back up the mountain, I'm going to need to get her settled soon and get going." He looked over to where Chewy lay napping, the loudness of the four of them not bothering his big furry ears at all.

"You know if it gets too late you guys can bunk here." Logan looked to Sera for confirmation and she nodded her head in agreement.

"Yeah...no. No thanks. I don't need to be exposed to whatever you guys get up to at night. Nope. Not going there."

"Fine, if you're that anxious, the keys are hanging on the hook by the door. Give me a minute and I'll get together a bag of linens and a few essentials." Sera jumped up and disappeared into the bedroom. When she came back, she had two giant bags full of items for the apartment. "You'll need to take her over to the general store, Jax. I've got her set up with quite a bit here, but I imagine there are some things she will want to pick out for herself."

"Oh, I'll be fine. I can't thank you enough, Sera. You, too, Logan. This is truly wonderful of you and I appreciate it more than you know."

"Just promise me you won't be a stranger while you're in town. Most of the time, if I'm not up here buried in a story, I'm down in the bar giving Logan a hard time or hanging with my girls. You are more than welcome to join us anytime you want."

"That's just lovely. Thank you again. I may take you up on that."

Charlie looked at Jax and smiled. "I guess I'm ready to go check out my new temporary home!"

Jax rose and held out a hand to her. "Well, then, let's do it."

Charlie wasn't sure what she expected, but the tidy little apartment was larger than she had pictured in her head. The furniture was a mix of different styles but for some reason, it worked well together. Sera told her the kitchen was fully equipped and Jax had been kind enough not to out her and her lack of cooking skills. Maybe, she thought, as she opened cabinet doors and looked at the contents, it was time to do some research and experimenting. Maybe if she studied hard enough she could teach herself to cook. Well, at least maybe she could get to the point where she wouldn't have to exist solely on restaurant takeout and cold cereal.

Jax was kind enough to help cart all her belongings up to the third-floor apartment. Between the two of them, it had only taken a couple of trips and now she was enjoying exploring her new living arrangements while Jax took Chewy for a quick walk. She was excited to unload her things and settle in, but the picture window looking out over the tiny town drew her and she found herself captivated, staring out at the snow-covered mountains in awe.

Buildings that could have just as easily been set in an 1800's western lined the streets and she itched to explore the small businesses. Not much traffic moved along the narrow roads, though the snow had been cleared, and she wondered if it was normal for Ouray. As she was standing there daydreaming, movement caught her eye and she realized it was Jax tugging Chewy along on a leash. She couldn't help but smile at the picture the two of them made together. A big guy and a big dog, both rough and rugged. They belonged in the mountains as if they had been made for it.

Was she made for mountain living, she wondered? Was this where she belonged? She just didn't know. She was still uncertain why the Colorado mountains had called to her, but she was here now, and she intended to see if it was where she was meant to be. For now? Well, for now, she knew it was where she wanted and needed to be. Time, she concluded, would tell her more on the meant-to-be front.

She was truly embarking on a new life and she was curious and excited to see what that life would become. There were many unknowns, many insecurities, and many questions. Hopefully, her time in the mountains would give her some of those answers and help her become the woman she truly wanted to be. The only thing she was certain of at this point was she never wanted to go back to the way things were.

When she heard the door to the apartment open and the happy barks of her new furry friend, she straightened, took a deep breath, and declared herself ready for whatever fate had in store for her.

Jax walked along behind the shopping cart, pushing it so Charlie would have her hands free to fill her cart until her heart was content. He couldn't help but marvel at how he'd gotten to this point. Four days earlier he'd had no idea who this woman was and now he was walking through the grocery with her helping her find items she would need to set up her apartment. The domestic implications made him want to cringe, but all it took was a look at the smile on her face for him to know there was no place else he'd rather be. He looked forward to getting to know her better, to helping her settle in, and make some friends.

He still couldn't get the thought out of his head that he needed to know what specifically made her run when she ran. There has to have been something, he thought. What was it after all those years that finally made her snap and say she'd had enough? Something triggered her response, something major, and he hoped she would feel comfortable enough with him someday to share.

He was lost in his thoughts, asking questions he had no answers to yet, when he heard a familiar voice. How, he thought, was he happy to hear it but cringing at the same damn time?

"Well, what have we here?"

"Ryder." Jax acknowledged his friend and grimaced before he turned to look at him. Oh, he wanted to knock the smug look off his face.

"More importantly, WHO have we here?" Ryder turned to face Charlie and when he did, that ineffable Ryder charm came oozing out of his pores. He held out his hand in greeting, "I'm Ryder, and you are?"

Charlie shook his hand and smiled at him with the same smile she offered everyone. So why, Jax wondered, did it ruffle his feathers to see her smiling at his friend?

"Hello. I'm Charlie."

"Interesting." He turned to Jax, "I didn't know there was a Charlie."

"Well, no, I suppose you wouldn't as she just got to town, Ry."

"I see. And how exactly did you two meet?" The implications in his voice once again had the hackles on the back of Jax's neck standing at attention.

"Oh! Well, that's easy." Charlie laughed. "I got lost in the snowstorm and fainted in his arms. He's been just wonderful to me. I don't know what I would have done without him."

"Oh, really?" Tongue in cheek, Ryder turned to him and Jax knew he was never going to live this down. "Well, I would just love to hear more."

"He's being kind enough to help me set up my new apartment."

"New apartment. So, you're planning on staying?"

"Well, for a while at least."

"Then I'm sure I'll be seeing you around. Perhaps even over at Logan's Bar & Grill. I'm there almost every night. In fact, I'll be there tonight if you're out and about."

"Well, I..."

"She's busy." Fuck! Jax couldn't believe he'd said that.

Once again, Ryder looked over at his friend, smirk on his face and mischief in his eyes, and Charlie, obviously unsure of what was happening, stood there with wide-eyed bewilderment written on her face.

"What I mean is, she's got things to do at her apartment. She probably isn't going to have time to go to Logan's tonight."

"Actually, Jax, I had been thinking it might be a good place for me to get dinner tonight. I'm sure I'll need a break and as I'm just getting settled in, it makes sense." Her tone took on the haughtyness with which she was raised and Jax felt well and truly put in his place.

"Again, interesting." Ryder looked from Jax to Charlie and back again. "Then it is my sincerest hope that I'm there when you decide to drop by. I've got to run." He turned then and walked away, but had only gotten a few steps when he called back over his shoulder, "Jax. I'll be seeing you."

Damn it, damn it, damn it! Jax knew he was in for the third degree and anticipating it, reached into his pocket and turned off his phone. This, he thought, was about to turn into the ribbing of all ribbings. Well, he thought, his friend could give him a hard time all he wanted. Jax was doing what anyone would do by giving Charlie a helping hand. There was nothing to be embarrassed about. Nope. Nothing at all.

Chapter Six

Charlie gave the soft flannel sheet a good shake and then spread it across the king-sized bed. She smoothed out the wrinkles and then reached for the thick, downy comforter Sera had supplied. If nothing else, she knew she would be toasty warm in her new home. Jax had offered to put away the groceries so she could work on settling in with the rest of her belongings. As she worked to unload her suitcase, she heard him moving around, opening and closing cabinets and drawers, stocking the pantry, and organizing all she bought at the grocery.

His kindness didn't surprise her so much as baffle her. Logically, she knew there were people like that in the world – just not in her world. At least, there weren't people like that in her old life. It was just one more thing she could add to the list of reasons she knew she was going to be happier turning away from the cold life she'd been brought up in. Good people, she thought, do exist. Friendly people do exist. And she was determined to make as many friends as possible.

Making these changes, leaving her old life behind, was bringing clarity like she'd never experienced before. Most of all, she knew she would never be forced or guilted into doing something she had no desire to do. Her parents had been pressuring her for months. She was their only hope for saving their social status, for keeping them from losing everything they had. Being on the brink of financial ruin had caused them to look to her to secure their future.

She could not, would not, do it.

She was a passionate person – at least she thought she was – and she knew the loveless marriage her parents were trying to force on her would bring nothing but misery and heartache. While she understood their need for security and social standing, she would never understand the careless way they were offering their only child up for auction. She had never felt love from them, or from anyone for that matter, so she supposed she shouldn't be surprised they were treating her as property rather than a beloved member of their family.

She had sat in Logan and Sera's living room that morning and seen the loving looks passed between them. She had watched the interactions between Jax and Sera – playful banter between siblings, and had witnessed the true bonds of friendship between Jax and Logan.

She wanted that. She wanted the friendships. She wanted the loving looks passed between two people who were meant to be together. She wanted a core group of people she could call her own. Most of all, she wanted to find love with a man who would cherish her for the rest of their lives.

One day, she thought, she would have it. It was simply unfortunate she'd been deprived of the most basic of needs her entire life.

With her hands on her hips, she looked around her new bedroom. She was completely unpacked and though the room was a bit sparse in decoration, it was hers – at least for now, and she loved it.

She walked into the living room and found Jax folding up the empty shopping bags and storing them in a drawer.

"All done! I guess I'm officially moved in."

"Excellent."

"I suppose you're anxious to head home. Jaxon, I can't thank you enough for – well, for everything. It means the world to me that you took me in when you didn't have to, but it means even more that you've helped me get started on this new path."

"It was the least I could do. And no, I'm not heading home tonight. It's getting late and I prefer to not travel snowy, icy roads in the dark."

"Oh, well, that makes sense, I suppose."

"I'll just bunk at Ryder's tonight."

"Alright then. I think I'm going to go to Logan's bar and have some dinner and you know, check things out."

"Mind if I join you?"

"Not at all! That would be perfect, actually. I'm still a bit uncomfortable sitting in a bar or restaurant by myself. I can do it if I absolutely have to, but something about it seems a little like putting myself on display. I'm used to hiding in corners, you know, being the quiet little mouse, the wallflower."

"First, there's nothing wrong with sitting by yourself to have a meal. Second, you should have never been put in a corner – by yourself or by anyone else. Third, I get all the free beer I want there. Dinner with a beautiful woman, wonderful conversation, and free beer? Count me in any day."

Charlie blushed. "Alright. Shall we?"

Jax reached for their coats and held hers out to her. "Let's do it."

For a Thursday night in the early days of the snowy season, Logan's Bar & Grill was hopping. The local crowd had reached their limit of being stuck inside their homes while the heavy snowfall had locked them away for a few days. Now that the roads were mostly clear they were ready to get out and socialize.

When Jax and Charlie walked into the bar it was packed. Classic rock pumped through the speakers and helped to drown out some of the noise from the crowd. The long mahogany bar gleamed in the soft lighting and the bar stools surrounding it were full. Logan stood behind the bar mixing drinks and pouring beer from an expansive array of taps.

A movement caught his eye, and Jax looked up to see Sera waiving them over to where she sat at a table in the back of the bar with their friend, Alex. He grabbed Charlie by the hand and successfully maneuvered them through the crowd and around the full tables to join them.

"Ladies," he greeted.

"Yay! I'm so glad you guys made it out tonight. Alex won't let me bore her with book talk. She keeps wanting to talk weddings. Don't get me wrong, I'm all about marrying Logan, but there are so many details to work out and I'm ready for a break. I have a feeling Charlie will indulge me. Oh! Alex, this is Charlie."

"Ah ha! Snowbound Charlie. It's nice to meet you. I see you survived your time with our dear Jaxon, here. I told you he's a good guy."

"It's wonderful to meet you, and thank you for easing my mind." She looked over to Jax and smiled. "He's been extremely kind and helpful to me."

"That's our guy! You won't find much better than the big guy there." Alex grinned cheekily at him.

"Yeah, yeah. I'm going to get a beer. What can I bring you, Charlie?"

"Oh, umm," Charlie looked at Sera and Alex's half-full drinks. "I'll have whatever that is."

Sera and Alex picked up their glasses and clinked them together, "Margaritas!"

"Logan's specialty. I'll be right back."

Charlie watched as he walked away and let himself through the passthrough separating the bar and patrons.

He picked up a mug and began to fill it with beer as he spoke to Logan, very much at home behind the bar. Jax's familiarity and the laid-back atmosphere pleased her.

"So, tell us, Charlie, what brings you to Ouray?" Alex took a sip of her drink and smiled over the rim.

"I'm not entirely sure. I decided to get away for a while and for some reason just felt drawn to Colorado."

"And where is it you normally call home?"

"Oh, umm..." Charlie looked around anxiously.

Alex leaned forward and crossed her arms on the table, scrutiny written on her face as she waited for an answer.

Sera playfully smacked Alex's arm. "Alex! Take off the cop hat, tuck away the badge, and relax for a while. She just met you and you're interrogating her. Let the girl breathe for Pete's sake!"

"You're right. Sorry. I tend to not be able to put the job aside sometimes."

"Just relax and have a little fun tonight, Charlie." Sera smiled kindly and immediately put Charlie at ease. "Something tells me you could use some of both."

"Alright. That sounds amazing!"

"You paying for that beer tonight?"

"You mean I gotta pay for a beer I fixed for myself? I mean, it's like I'm doing the work for you, man. It's like I'm an employee."

"Alright," Logan teased, "if you're working for me, you know the rules. No drinking on the job."

"Fuck."

"Got ya." Logan began pouring and mixing Charlie's margarita. "So, how's your girl settling in?"

"Whoa. Hold up. She's not my girl."

Logan raised his eyebrows as he looked over at his friend. "What?"

"All I'm saying is you're going above and beyond with her – more than I've seen you do with someone in too many years to count – maybe even ever. Kinda seems like she COULD be your girl. One day. Maybe."

"Dude. Don't make me clock you. I'm a good guy. She needed help – I gave her help. She needs friends – I'm a friendly guy and," he nodded his head to where the trio sat, "I'm helping her make more friends. End of discussion."

"Alright, here. Take your friend her drink and get out from behind my bar."

"Yeah, yeah. Let me just top off my beer so I don't have to come back here and disturb Tom Cruise while he's entertaining the crowd with his mixologist prowess for a bit. Mix those cocktails, Maverick."

"You're combining movie references! Go! Just Go!" Logan laughed at his friend and shook his head.

Jax carried their drinks through the crowd, dodging waitresses and patrons as he went. He'd just given Charlie her drink and sat down when he looked up to see Ryder walking through the door and headed their direction.

"Damn it." Alex rolled her eyes and took a long sip from her margarita.

"Come on, Alex." Sera looked at her friend exasperated. "You either need to get the fuck over it or you and Ryder need to finally sit down and talk. This has gone on long enough."

"Not happening. Neither option."

Jax grimaced, "She has a point, Alex."

"Hey! No ganging up on the wronged party. That's just rude."

"Then put on your pleasant face, at the very least, and don't ruin the evening for our new friend." Sera chided.

"Yeah, yeah. Fine." Alex smiled and blinked her eyes. "Better?"

"Bitch."

"Slut."

"Whore."

"I love you."

"I love you, too."

Throughout the exchange between Sera and Alex, Jax couldn't help but watch Charlie's reaction. Amusement. Shock. Wistfullness. Oh, Little Rabbit, he thought, you have so much to learn and experience. He smiled inwardly as he realized he was looking forward to watching her learn, grow, and bloom.

After a series of stops at various tables to say hello, Ryder finally reached them, and grabbing an empty chair from a neighboring table, wedged his way between Sera and Charlie. "Ladies," he grinned, then nodded at Jax, "asshole." Then he pointedly looked toward Alex and smirked. "Alex."

"As always, a fucking pleasure, Ryder." Alex rolled her eyes.

"That's enough." Jax looked back and forth between his friends. "This is Charlie's first night in town. You two aren't going to ruin it for her over something that happened more than a decade ago. Fucking let it go for the night."

Alex and Ryder both held their hands up in surrender. "Fine, fine."

A waitress came and sat a beer in front of Ryder and conversation began to flow between the five of them.

"Well, I," Ryder smiled at Charlie, "would love to hear more about how you ended up with the big guy here, and," he looked at Jax with mischief in his eyes, "your time spent together during snowmageddon."

"Oh, Jax has been truly wonderful to me. You see, Ryder, I was completely turned around on those mountain roads and hadn't paid attention to how quickly the snow was falling. I was just dazzled by how beautiful it was. Before I knew it, it got dark and I became even more discombobulated. It seems I'm directionally challenged, even with GPS." She rolled her eyes and laughed softly. "It wasn't too long before I began having trouble driving in the snow. When I got stuck I did the only thing I could think of and took off walking to the nearest structure shown on the GPS. As it turns out," she smiled at Jax, "the nearest structure was Jaxon's home. He has been wonderful to me. You were right, Alex," she smiled, "I didn't have anything to worry about when it came to trusting Jax."

"Like I said when you called, he's one of the good ones."

"Yes," she turned and smiled wistfully at him, "I do believe you're correct. He's definitely a trouvaille." When everyone seated at the table looked at her in confusion, she laughed and explained. "A trouvaille is something or someone lovely discovered by chance; a lucky find."

Jax chuckled at the incredulous looks darting around the table. "She's a linguaphile."

"Oh! Oh! I know that one!" Sera perked up. "Well, that explains so much! You love languages. Yes, I can see where you would enjoy reading as much as you do. I do believe you and I are going to get along well and become fast friends!"

Conversation began to flow effortlessly between them. It wasn't long before Jax found himself looking at the bottom of his empty mug.

"Come on Ryder," Jax began, "let's go bug Logan and get these ladies another round of drinks."

When just the three women remained, Sera and Alex leaned toward each other conspiratorily. "Well, what do you think of Jax, Charlie?"

"Oh, I, umm, like I said, he's wonderful."

"Yes. But what do you really think of him?" Alex teased unmercifully.

"I'm not certain I know what you're getting at."

"What my best friend here is trying to say without saying is, do you think you might be interested romantically in my brother?"

"I didn't say a damn word about romance. I was leaning more toward the sexual side of things. Do you think you might be interested in him sexually?"

"Alex!"

"What? You know I don't hold back."

"Well, I don't suppose I've given it much thought. I mean, we just met." Then the image of Jax, naked, fresh from the shower floated through her mind.

"Oh, no you don't. See that look on her face, Sera. Something happened. I know that look. I know that look very, very well."

"Umm..."

"Spill it, girlfriend."

"There was an incident." Charlie felt her face flush and quickly looked down to where her hands rested on the table and began to nervously wring them together.

"Ooh! An incident! I do love me some incidents."

"Alex..."

"What? Don't lie, bitch. You know you love incidents, too. Otherwise, you wouldn't put so damn many of them in your books."

"Got me. Carry on, Charlie."

"Yesterday morning, well... Oh, goodness. I don't know if I can talk about things like this." The rose color that tinged her cheeks brightened further as she glanced left and right and nervously bit her bottom lip, too shy to carry on with her thoughts out loud.

"You can. You really can." Sera rolled her eyes at Alex.

"Alright. He had just gotten out of the shower. I...I didn't realize he was in there. I thought he had already started working and was busy in his office. I just...walked right in on him. Oh, my God! I was mortified!" Charlie's face flamed as she hid behind her hands in embarrassment. "Even worse? I was...oh, God. I was so turned on. He has an amazing body. He's all tattooed and muscley and thick and his," she looked around to make sure nobody was listening in on their conversation and then lowered her voice to a whisper, "penis is..."

"Whoa..." Sera held up her hands to halt the conversation and shook her head from side to side in horror.

"Excuse me," Alex interrupted at the same time. "What did you just say? Did you say 'penis'? Is that seriously the word she used?" Alex looked at Sera for confirmation.

"Yes. That's the word she used. And I'm sorry, but this is my brother we're talking about. I can't talk about his...appendages. At least I can't talk about THAT one!"

Ignoring Sera's discomfort, Charlie looked around in confusion. "What's wrong with penis?"

Sera opened her mouth to explain but was cut off by Alex. "I've got this," she smirked at Sera and wagged a finger to stop her. "Are we in anatomy class?"

Charlie looked around wild-eyed. "No."

"Are you a pre-pubescent teenager giggling over your first glimpse of the statue of David?"

"Umm...no."

"Are you a grown-ass fucking adult capable of using descriptively appealing, sexually pleasing terms to describe body parts?"

"Yes, I suppose I am." Once again Charlie looked around, this time shyly, and as she did, her face turned beet red once more.

"Well then, here's what we're going to use instead: cock, dick, or schlong. I might even go for magic wand, gear shift, or joystick. But we are never, and I do mean never ever, going to use the term penis again. Okay?"

"Umm, okay."

"And for the love of God, I better not ever hear you use the word vagina!"

"Oh, God. That's enough, Alex." Sera began to laugh. "Bless your heart, Charlie. You'll have to excuse her. She can be very crass. She always makes a good point, but she is most definitely crass."

"That's just one of the reasons you love me." Alex batted her eyes at Sera.

"True, but I've had a lifetime to know you and know your personality. Charlie has just met you."

"I don't mind crass. I'm just not used to it. Or, I'm not used to it outside of books. I've never had girlfriends I could be open with like this before. It's a new experience for me."

"Well, welcome to the club, little sister. We're glad to have you and we'll get you out of that shell in no time."

"Here, here!" Sera picked up her glass and downed the last of her margarita.

"And here come the guys. I guess we will have to table talk of Jax's cock to another time."

Sera swallowed and almost choked, "Alex! Damn it!"

"Got ya!"

Charlie sighed and smiled. "I love the banter between the two of you. I can tell you truly love each other. It's fascinating!"

Jax and Ryder sat drinks in front of them all and rejoined the discussion. The five of them stayed until the bar shut down and then helped Logan close up for the night. When they parted ways, promises to get together again soon echoed all around.

Jax hooked the leash on Chewy and stood. He had delivered Charlie back to her new home and rounded up everything he'd brought with him for the dog.

"I guess I'll go invade Ryder's sofa. Are you going to be alright here by yourself?"

"Of course. I'll be fine." Charlie smiled up at him.

"Alright. Well, then, I guess I'll see you around. Promise me you'll call me if something comes up, okay?"

"I will." He turned to go and when he felt her hand on his arm stopping him from leaving, his heart fluttered in his chest. "Jax. Thank you again. You, well, as much as I love words, I simply can't think of any better way to say this, but you may very well have saved my life. I can't thank you enough."

"It's what anyone would do."

"No. Not just anyone." She stood on tiptoe then and placed a gentle kiss on his cheek. "Goodnight, Jax."

Torn between leaving and grabbing her and diving into the perfect bow of her mouth, Jax took a deep breath and smiled down at her. "Goodnight, Charlie."

Chapter Seven

"Rise and shine, asshole."

"Fuck right the fuck off, Ryder." Jax never opened his eyes as his gravelly, sleep-filled voice berated his friend for waking him up.

"No can do. I've got a court case in an hour which means I need to get my ass on the road. And as much as I love your bear cub here, I don't have time to take him out for a piss."

"Fuck. Why did I want a dog again?"

"I'm going to go with you're a lonely old codger and needed some entertainment to keep you from going completely bat-shit crazy up at that cabin by yourself."

"I'm going to say it again, dude. Fuck. Off."

Ryder laughed and kicked the bottom edge of the sofa." Coffee is fresh, bro. I'm out."

When Jax heard the door close, he blinked his eyes open. When he felt hot breath on his cheek he turned and found himself looking straight into a pair of curious black eyes.

"Yeah, yeah. I get it. I'm getting up. Patience, my guy. I gotta piss, too, and while we could both normally do that outside, I can't while we're in town." With that, he sat up and began his day.

An hour later Jax climbed the stairs outside Charlie's new apartment, Chewy hot on his heels. He raised his hand to knock on the door when the unmistakable odor of scorched food reached his nose. He shook his head and began to knock. When the door swung open and smoke rolled out, Charlie stood on the other side looking to Jax for help and waving her hand in front of her face.

"Oh! Thank God! I..." Just then the smoke alarm began to blare and concern for what exactly he was about to find made Jax barrel through the door, pushing past Charlie in his haste and knocking her into the wall with a thud.

When Jax entered the kitchen the smell of burnt food and the smoky haze in the air began to make him cough. The charred remains of whatever she attempted to cook sat in a scorched pan on the stovetop. The door to the microwave stood ajar and more smoke billowed out of the opening. He took a quick look to make sure the appliances were turned off and then went to the smoke detector and pressed the button to silence the screaming alarm. Then cocking an eyebrow at Charlie and trying his best to hide his amusement, he opened the window over the kitchen sink. Hopefully, he thought, the smoke and stench would clear out quickly.

"Good morning, Little Rabbit. I see you've been trying your hand at cooking."

"Umm, yeah. I think I failed."

"Without a doubt, I can say you got a big, red F on this assignment. Do you want to walk me through what you were trying to do here?"

"I scrambled some eggs."

Jax looked at the mountain of yellow and black currently solidifying in the skillet on the stove and winced.

"And when that failed I thought maybe some oatmeal would be a good option."

He turned then to look inside the microwave and saw the problem. He ran a hand over his face in disbelief.

"Alright. I'm going to have to give you a few lessons."

"I thought I could figure it out. I watched you when we were at the cabin and you made it look so easy. Why wasn't it easy, Jax?" Dismay crept into her voice and when he looked into her eyes and saw the tears she was desperately trying not to let fall, his heart tripped in his chest. He walked to her and wrapped his arms around her, enveloping her in a comforting hug.

"Hey... It's alright. I promise it's okay. Everything is going to be okay. Look at me." Charlie eased back from his large frame and looked up into his eyes. "You've got this. All of this."

"I do?"

"Yeah. You do. It's just going to take time."

"I don't even know where to begin, Jax."

"You've already started. You took the first step, the hardest step, and it was a doozy. Walking away from the only life you've ever known to live the life you truly want is huge. Now, we just have to backtrack a bit and take some baby steps to get you the skills you need to travel down the next path on your own."

She sniffled and laid her head on his chest once more as his arms pulled her close again. He held her until he felt her spine stiffen and knew she had resolved to figure things out. She pulled out of his arms, squared her shoulders, and walked to the stove.

"Alright. What did I do wrong?"

"My best guess with the eggs is that you had your heat too high and you didn't use any cooking spray on the pan."

"Cooking spray?"

"Oh, boy!" Jax chuckled. "And," he stepped to the microwave and grimaced, "sweetheart, there are certain things you cannot do when cooking in a microwave. Using a metal bowl is one of them. You're actually pretty lucky you didn't start a fire or blow up the microwave."

"What?!?" The horror that rang out in her voice made him wince. "Oh, my God! Oh, my God!" She began to pace back and forth in the tiny kitchen.

"Hey, now... The good news is you caught it before things got bad."

"I can't do this."

"Yes, you can."

"What if I had burned down the apartment? The building?" Back and forth she went, chewing on the tip of her thumb as she contemplated the worst-case scenario.

"Charlie."

"Sera would never forgive me. I'd have to look for another place to live. I could have put lives in danger, including mine. What was I thinking? I can't do this, Jax."

"Charlie!" He raised his voice to get her attention, impatience and frustration echoing through his censure. She stopped pacing and stared at him in alarm, wild-eyed and frightened.

"Charlie. Little Rabbit. Look at me. You CAN do this. You will do this. I will help you. Logan, Sera, and Alex will help you. Hell, even Ryder will help you. Don't give up on day one, problem one."

"You think so?"

"I know so."

"Alright. You're right. I just need some instruction. I can do this."

"That's the spirit. Now, how about we let the apartment air out a bit while we go over to the cafe and get some breakfast? We'll do that then we'll come back here and I'll give you a quick cooking lesson or two. Sound good?"

She nodded her head and smiled, "Yes. That sounds wonderful."

"Oh! This is the most adorable cafe!" Charlie gave the outside of the building an appreciative look as she studied the facade. She'd traveled the world over and eaten at cafes and bistros in every city she visited. Paris? Rome? They were fascinating, romantic, and sophisticated. Though she appreciated the opportunities to travel and experience the culture, she could already tell she much preferred this small cafe in the tiny little town nestled in the mountains.

The homey touches with a Western feel made her heart swell with belonging.

Jax held the door for her and then ushered her to a small table, pulling out a chair for her before skirting to the other side and making himself comfortable. His large frame dwarfed the chair but even though he made the furniture look small, he somehow fit in perfectly with the atmosphere. She wondered exactly how it was he appeared to belong no matter where they were. It didn't seem to matter if he was lazing in his cabin, pouring beer behind Logan's bar, or sitting at a bistro table with a glass top etched with cowboys riding horses and roping cattle. He just fit.

She wasn't certain she fit anywhere. She'd never been comfortable at her boarding school, had always felt out of place at those other cafes, and most certainly had never felt as if she belonged in the mansion she once occupied. She couldn't say "lived in" as she never felt she had lived while she was there. While she couldn't say for sure she would ever belong in Ouray, she at least felt more comfortable here than anywhere else in her life.

It gave her a sense of hope for her future.

"You can't go wrong with anything you order here. Trust me, I've tried it all."

"Oh, so you eat here often?"

"Actually, no. But I've tried everything on the menu because I was one of the test subjects growing up."

"I'm sorry. I'm confused."

Jax laughed and looked toward the back of the cafe where a woman with gray hair stood filling a tray with coffee mugs and breakfast plates. She looked up and seeing Jax and Charlie at a table, smiled before returning to her work.

"The cafe belongs to my mother. She made me and Sera try everything before she added it to the menu. That's her," he nodded toward the woman who had been behind the counter, "and she will be walking this way in three, two, one..."

"Jaxon. I heard you were in town." The woman, tall, statuesque, and beautiful, leaned over to place a kiss on top of her son's head before turning her attention to Charlie. "And you must be the famous Charlie I've been hearing about."

Hearing about? Oh God! Charlie was certain her face flushed crimson under the scrutiny. "I'm not sure what you've heard, but yes, I'm Charlie. It's lovely to meet you."

"Oh, now... I've heard nothing but good things. Sera stopped by this morning to have breakfast with me. You just missed her, actually. I already know what Jax will want to eat, but what can I get you?"

"Oh, well, I..."

"Just double the order, Ma." Charlie looked at Jax with bewilderment. Just how, she wondered, did the man know what she wanted to eat? What if she didn't like whatever it was?

"Alright, then. It won't take long and I'll have some coffee right out to you." With a smile at her son and a curious lift of her eyebrow, she turned and headed back into the kitchen.

Charlie found herself staring at Jax incredulously.

"Trust me. You're going to love it."

She rolled her eyes at him. "Okay, but, you know, I might have wanted to at least look at a menu."

"Understood. Just have a bit of faith. Your first visit here demands what I've ordered. Next time, we'll do it your way."

"Next time?"

Jax grinned, "Yeah. Next time. I feel certain we'll be back if your cooking abilities don't show drastic improvement."

"Not funny, Jax." She wasn't sure whether to be thankful he was looking out for her or offended that he'd called her on her inabilities.

"It's kind of funny." The teasing laughter in his eyes immediately put her at ease.

It only took her a moment to smile back at him, and when two steaming mugs of coffee were set in front of them, she decided to just go with the flow. New town. New experiences. New life.

Everything was going to be alright.

Charlie sat back in her chair and placed a hand on her stomach. She didn't think she had ever eaten so much in her entire life! When Jax's mother had placed their food in front of them, Charlie had stared in disbelief. Their plates were piled with an array of choices. A short stack of sweet cream cheese pancakes topped with a berry compote was the main attraction. A small pyramid of frittatas sat to one side of the pancakes and on the other side lay a stack of dark-chocolate-dipped bacon. Her mouth had immediately begun to water in anticipation, and when Jax's mother returned to the table with a basket of lavender-infused lemon mini muffins, her mouth had popped open in awe.

"I don't think I can move. Oh, my God! That was simply amazing!"

"Aren't you glad you chose to trust me?"

She paused as she studied the man before her. Trust had never come easy – her family had ruined that ideation - and their most recent commands and demands had further destroyed her ability to believe and have faith in anyone.

But for some reason, though she had only known Jax a matter of days, she trusted him more than she'd ever trusted anyone. He had proved and kept proving himself worthy of her faith and trust.

"Yes. Yes, I'm glad I trusted you – with breakfast and everything else. Thank you, Jaxon. I can't possibly tell you what it means to me to have found a friend like you."

One corner of his mouth lifted in a smile as he reached into the basket and grabbed the last muffin. "Be right back." He popped the sweetness in his mouth then grabbed their dirty dishes and carted them to the kitchen. She watched then as he grabbed his mother in a fierce hug. Then, with laughter in his eyes, he held up a hand to stop her as she spoke to him in a hushed whisper. Shaking his head at his mother, he leaned over, kissed her on the cheek, and returned to where Charlie sat.

"Shall we go give you a few cooking lessons?"

"Alright. Don't you have work you need to be doing, though?"

"One of the advantages of being my own boss. I get to choose when and how much I feel like working."

"Well, if you're certain, a few basics would be wonderful."

"Let's do it." He offered his hand to help her up and with her hand snugly caught in his, ushered her out the door and down the street to her apartment.

Jax cranked the heater in his Jeep and then reached over to ruffle the fur on Chewy's neck. Grabbing his phone from his pocket, he pulled up one of his favorite playlists and punched the Jeep into four-wheel drive. He turned up the volume and began rocking out to his all-time favorite band, Shinedown. He was in a great mood.

As he drove and sang along to the music, he began thinking over the past few days and the time he had spent with Charlie. She fascinated him. Her beauty was obviously a big draw. The old Hollywood glamour she exuded without even trying was enough to make any man drool. Her intelligence blew him away. He'd always found a woman with a knowledgable and seeking mind attractive. But for some reason, it was her shy curiosity that drew him like a homing beacon. She might not know all she wanted from life, but he knew she wanted to live, to experience so many things life had to offer. He also knew she was too timid to act on many of those desires and experiences without some encouragement. Not only did he want to encourage her, but he was finding he truly liked the idea of being right there with her when she had those experiences. He wanted to witness her reactions firsthand.

He wasn't certain what the turning point had been for him to start thinking of her as more than an uninvited houseguest and new friend, but so far all roads were leading to the moment she walked in on him getting out of the shower and seeing the reaction she had to his naked body. That one moment where her curiosity overpowered her shyness had flipped a switch in him and he was finding he had no desire to flick the switch and turn it off again.

For some reason, her timid spirit and accompanying bashful blush seriously turned him on.

Shyness had never been on the table for him before. The women he hooked up with all knew the score. They were bold and brazen. They got together, had their fun, then went their separate ways. But Charlie's shyness was endearing and sexy as hell.

He wanted to be her friend – Lord knew she needed friends. Being friends was a good thing, a great thing even. Friends. Yep, he wanted to be her friend.

Oh, hell, he thought. Who am I kidding? He wanted to take a big bite out of her and savor each and every moment. He wanted to show her what she'd been missing out on all these years, and he wanted to show her just how truly amazing it could be. He could do that and still be her friend, right?

Yeah. Friends could be lovers and lovers could be friends. You just need to lay a good foundation and have an honest discussion about things before you jump into anything.

It's all about the approach, he thought. Time. She definitely needed time to adjust to her new life, her new outlook on that life, and the new people she was bringing into her life. For now, he decided, he would keep things friendly and keep his hands to himself.

For now.

But, first things first, he thought. He wanted to know more about her family. He wanted to know exactly why she had decided to run when she did. What was it that finally pushed her over the edge toward freedom?

His fingers got that familiar itch to be behind his command center. As soon as he got home he had plans to dig in and he wasn't surfacing until he had answers.

Chapter Eight

Charlie checked and re-checked the settings on the washing machine. She was certain she had things set correctly. Well, almost certain, she thought.

After a beginner's cooking lesson, Jax had departed, leaving her to her own devices. Now she stood questioning herself in front of a simple machine that scared the living daylights out of her.

Today was the first time she'd been by herself without something to distract her since she'd run from her former life. She'd had the driving, the exhaustion, and the snow to deal with up until now. She found she hardly knew what to do with herself and her new-found freedom. She had read for a while and had even turned on the television for a bit. But, eventually, antsiness had won out and she'd decided to rearrange things around the apartment to make things more to her liking.

The dirty clothes she had piled in the lone recliner in her bedroom the day before had grown a set of eyes at some point in the short time she'd been there. Each time she'd gone in and out of the bedroom while she was moving things, she felt as if she was being watched. Each time she passed it, the mound grew, judging her and her ineptness at maneuvering day-to-day life. She finally reached a point where she fully believed it was going to crawl out of the chair in a horror movie move and slide across the floor, chasing her menacingly to hold her accountable for her non-action.

Eventually, she had given in, squared her shoulders, and gathered the pile. She had started to just throw everything in the washer and hope for the best, but after her disastrous experience with cooking breakfast, she decided to take the time to Google the proper way to wash clothes, and what settings to use on the washer and dryer. Now, as she pushed the start button on the daunting machine, she hoped and prayed she had understood everything and remembered correctly.

When water started flowing into the beast, she breathed a sigh of relief. Now, she thought, I just have to wait. A few moments passed before she realized she was standing there staring at the machine, and she began to laugh at herself. She returned to the living room, picked up her book, and snuggled into the corner of the sofa, satisfied she was being productive even as she took time for herself. But it wasn't long before she gave up, and taking her book with her, returned to the laundry room and sat on the floor in front of the machine to keep an eye on it. Just in case.

She was deep into a spicy scene when a loud buzz emanated from the machine. She yelped and fumbled her book as she jumped up, heart racing, and cautiously peeked at the readout. When she saw a yellow light next to the word 'done,' she breathed a sigh of relief. She had just gotten the dryer going and walked into the kitchen when she heard the sound of a text notification echo throughout the apartment. Before she could pick up her phone, another notification came through making her wonder what was so urgent. She opened her screen expecting it to be Jax but was pleasantly surprised to see it was from Sera.

Sera

> Girls' night with Alex and our friend Val. No men allowed! You in?

> You'll love Val! She's Amazing!

Charlie
> Really?

Sera
> I've never done anything like that before. Absolutely! Count me in! What time? Where?

Charlie
> What do I wear?

Sera
> Oooooh! Fun! Hold that thought...

> Okay. Just checked with them. Wear something sexy – remember it's cold. 6 pm. Just be ready. We'll come and get you!

Charlie
> Sexy?

> I don't have anything sexy!

Sera
> What???

Charlie
> Long story...

> **Sera**
> Hmm… Okay. Change of plans. I'll come over early and bring some stuff. Alex and Val can pick us up.

> **Charlie**
> Oh! Well…uh… Okay. I guess I'll see you in a bit!

> **Sera**
> Eeek! This is going to be so much fun! TTYL!

Charlie laid the phone down and seeing what time it was, hurried to the shower. Excitement made her giddy. Friends! She was finally making friends!

The joy she felt threatened to overflow her heart. Tears threatened to fall but she fought them back instead, preferring to just be happy and live in the moment.

By the time she finished with her shower and stood before the mirror, towel wrapped around her body, another tied in a turban to catch the drips from her wet hair, she was walking on air. She looked at herself in the mirror and smiled. Then, letting her joy take over, she began to shake her hips in a happy dance.

She refused to let anyone or anything ruin her life ever again. This was it. This was all she'd ever hoped for.

New life. New friends. New outlook.

"Well, Charlotte Grace. It's about damn time!"

When the knock on her door came an hour later, Charlie rushed to open it with a smile beaming from ear to ear.

"You're here!"

"Well, of course! I told you I was coming!" Sera hurried inside, arms loaded with garment bags.

"I know. It's just, this is all so new to me. I kept checking my phone to make sure I hadn't dreamed the whole conversation."

"Girl..." Sera shook her head in disbelief, "someone truly did a number on you. Don't you worry, we'll build up that confidence. Now, let's decide on something for you to wear. To the bedroom!"

Sera spread the options on the bed and then removed her coat. Stunned, all Charlie could do was stand there with her mouth agape. The dress Sera wore seemed barely there in her opinion and looked as if it was a second skin.

"Holy crap, Sera! You look stunning! I thought you said to remember to dress for warmth. I don't know how you plan on keeping warm in that! And, umm, does Logan know you're wearing that?"

Laughter bubbled out of her new friend at her naivety. "Yes, Logan knows I'm wearing this. In fact, he helped me fasten the straps – after he removed them and had his way with me, that is."

Charlie's eyes widened and a blush crept up her face. "Well, alright then. I guess you do live out some of the things you write about."

"Oh, absolutely, I do! To respond to the warmth part of your concerns, I wore a coat, didn't I?" She bubbled with laughter and Charlie couldn't help but join in. "Now, let's take a look and see if we can find something a little more," she looked Charlie up and down, "okay, a lot more sexy than what you're wearing."

Garment bags were unzipped and each option soon lay spread across the bed in an array of sequins, straps, and barely there material.

"This one." Sera picked up a dress and smiled as she nodded at Charlie. "And," she squinted her eyes thoughtfully, "pull the hair up. Show off that incredible neckline."

"Oh, my goodness! I... I can't wear that!" Charlie looked at all the options Sera had chosen with dismay. "I can't wear any of those! I'm not built for those!"

"Girl! Yes, you can, and oh, yes, you are!"

"I don't know, Sera."

"Trust me."

Charlie wasn't sure what to do. The dresses were gorgeous but so much sexier than anything she'd ever worn.

Her super-conservative parents had always insisted she wear clothing from high-end designers and nothing too revealing. After all, what if she were to marry someone in politics? There was her reputation to think of and in turn, the reputation of her future husband. Her thoughts raced until an image of Jaxon appeared in her mind and acted as a stop sign. Suddenly, it dawned on her she was still fighting the image and mindset she was running from. Damn it! She refused to live that way any longer.

With renewed determination and a steely resolve, Charlie nodded at Sera. "Alright. I'll trust you."

"Hot damn! This dress, for sure! I'll just step out and wait for Alex and Val. This night is going to be epic!"

As soon as she was alone, she sat on the bed and exhaled. She could do this. She WAS doing this. She looked down at the dress in her lap and a wide grin spread across her face. Alright, she thought. It's time for the new and improved Charlotte Grace to make her appearance.

Fifteen minutes later Charlie opened the door to her bedroom to a chorus of whistles and the nervousness that had snuck in on her as she'd dressed vanished without a trace.

Charlie wasn't sure what she expected, but the old-timey saloon most certainly hadn't been it. Wanting the opportunity to get out of Ouray for a change, the women had decided to travel north to Ridgway for their night out. The short drive had been full of laughs and camaraderie. It was obvious to her the three women sharing stories had known and loved each other for a lifetime.

It hadn't taken long for her to feel as if she were a part of things as they wouldn't let her stay silent long. The immediate affection she had felt when she had met Sera and Alex the day before had instantly appeared with Val, as well. Charlie was giddy with happiness. She'd missed out on so much throughout her life and she was determined to make up for lost time.

The bar was hopping and the restaurant was busy, too. They managed to grab a table and it wasn't long before they each had a margarita in their hand.

"To Charlie!"

"What? Why?"

"Why not? You are our newest friend, our newest confidant, and the newest member of our crew. You are and will always be welcome to join us on girls' night!

"Oh, wow! I'm not sure what to say. I'm so glad to have met all of you and so thankful for you just opening your arms this way and inviting me in. I've never, and I do mean never, had that before. I can't possibly tell you how much it means to me."

"To Charlie?"

"Yes! To me and my new friends and new life!"

"Here! Here!"

Glasses clinked and first sips were had.

"Oh, yeah! The bartender hit these just right tonight!"

Alex chuckled, "Don't let Logan hear you say that, Sera. You know he prides himself on his margarita skills."

"Oh, I'm not worried about him. Besides, he prides himself on quite a bit." She snorted as she giggled and wiggled her eyebrows at her friends.

"Well, from what I see, that pride is well-deserved." Charlie slapped a hand over her mouth in horror. Had she really just said that?

The table went quiet as they all turned to look at Charlie in astonishment.

It was Sera who broke through the shock of the moment first. "Ha! See!" She laughed, "I told you she fits right in with us!"

"Agreed!" Val and Alex echoed.

"I can't believe I said that."

"Oh, no. No apologies! That was perfect! Relax honey! That is exactly the kind of banter that makes girls' night so damn much fun!"

The tension that had built in Charlie's stomach released like a popped balloon. She immediately relaxed and began to feel as if she truly belonged with the three beautiful women before her.

They were on their second margaritas when Alex could no longer take it. "Alright. Tell us about Charlie."

"Oh, well. Let me see." She paused for a moment to gather her thoughts. She knew she could trust her new friends, but part of her still worried – especially with Alex being a police officer. How much could she tell them? Should she tell them everything? Not quite yet, she decided. In time, maybe, but everything was still so new. She felt she needed a bit more space from her old life first. "Alright. I grew up on the East Coast – I guess you can hear that in my voice. I'm an only child. And a little less than a week ago I left everything I've ever known and took off driving across the country on the most epic road trip in an effort to find myself. Here I am."

"And your parents?" Alex questioned as she took a sip of her margarita.

"I'm not close with them at all. If you don't mind, I'd rather talk about most anything else than to talk about them."

"That," Sera looked pointedly at Alex, "is not a problem."

"Well, what about..."

"Alex!"

"Come on, Alex." Val looked at her and shook her head. "Let her tell us what she wants to tell us when she wants to tell us."

"Fine. Fine. I'm sorry, Charlie. Sometimes I just can't turn off my inquisitiveness. Hazard of the job."

"It's alright. Seriously. Just," she ducked her head shyly, "give me a bit more time, maybe?"

"Alright."

"Thank you. Thank all of you. Tonight has been amazing. You don't know how much I appreciate you all for including me."

"Oh, little sister, the night is young! Sit back and hold on tight!"

Charlie couldn't hold back her beaming smile. This, she thought, is what it's all about.

Jax stood and stretched. His neck was stiff and there was a mild ache in his lower back. He'd been behind his command center for hours digging up everything he could find on Charlie and her family. When he'd found all he thought he could find easily, he began to dig deeper, venturing into the dark web to do a deep dive into the family, their background, and their financials. He now knew, or at least he thought he knew, part of the reason Charlie had finally gathered her courage and escaped the cold, heartless world she'd been born into.

He'd been digging for about two hours when he'd found the first indication of what might be wrong. Under layers and layers of false trails and lies he'd found the truth – the Abbingdons were about to lose it all.

A series of bad investments – extremely bad investments - had started the ball rolling on the downward spiral of the Abbingdon fortune. The part that had taken him so long to dig up was that it went back a couple of generations. It seemed Charlie's great-grandfather had been the one to take the initial fall from grace. Scandal had rocked their family and been swept under the rug. An illegitimate child, a huge payoff, a bad investment in an overseas company to try to repair the hit to their finances from the payoff... It was as if a door had opened at that point and a deluge of information came flooding out.

Somehow, even though the family coffers had been slowly dwindling, the Abbingdon's had managed to maintain their social status. This had caught Jax's interest and his digging had finally revealed a pattern.

Charlie's great-grandfather had arranged his oldest daughter's marriage, and on the day of the wedding, a hefty sum had appeared in their ledger, divided amongst multiple accounts in an attempt to hide their illicit procurement. It had happened again with their other daughter. Again, he'd found evidence of a payoff on the day of the wedding. Once Jax connected those dots, it was easy to see the pattern in the next generation. With each marriage and subsequent payment, there had been more and more bad investments. Every time they would get a bit of a reprieve, something would tank and their funds would disappear.

Now it was Charlie's turn, or at least as best he could tell it was. Only, with Charlie's parents it wasn't only a series of bad investments they were fighting, it was also a gambling addiction her father couldn't seem to step away from.

When Jax had put everything together and it finally began to sink in that they were auctioning off their daughter, the beautiful creature he'd shared his home with and had quickly grown fond of, he'd become livid. He would not let her be a victim of their scheming ways. He would protect her and her identity at all costs.

Part of that protection had come in the form of trying to trace her movements as she'd driven across the United States. She'd been careful, but, as he knew which route she took, he'd been able to catch a trace or two of her trip. Traffic cams and security footage from hotels had now been deleted and evidence of her escape route was hidden to the best of his ability.

Jax was determined to keep her safe and help her take root in her new life. He just hoped she would decide to stay in Ouray long-term.

"Chewy! Let's go out, bud. One more piss before we turn in, okay?"

The woof he received in answer was interrupted by a text tone sounding from his phone. He looked at the clock on the wall in confusion, curious as to who would be texting at midnight. When he picked up his phone and saw the text from Sera, he smiled. But when he opened the message and was greeted with a photograph of four beautiful women wearing skimpy dresses, tits and asses barely covered by sequined materials, he almost dropped his phone.

The woman he saw in the photo wasn't the timid and somewhat frightened woman he'd shared his home with.

No, the woman he was looking at now bore the markings of a sexy siren out on the prowl for a good time. As much as he loved looking at her dressed to kill like she was, he was also livid.

What had his sister done with his Little Rabbit?

Chapter Nine

Jax
> WTF, Sera?

Sera
> Doesn't she look great?!?

> We're having the best time!

Jax
> Where are you?

Sera
> Relax! Girls' night in Ridgway.

> We're only a little tipsy. Promise!

Jax
> Is she okay?

Sera

She? You mean Charlie?

Jax

Who else?

Sera

Are those protective vibes I'm getting from you, big bro?

Jax

I'm just concerned.

She's been a bit sheltered.

Sera

Sure. If you say so.

Jax

Damn it! Answer me.

Is she alright?

Sera

> LOL! Yes, Jaxon. She is fine. We're heading back to Ouray. Breathe. Your girl has had a wonderful evening and let loose a bit. It was just what she needed.

> I'll let her know you asked about her...

Jax
> Don't you fucking dare!

Sera
> Toooooooo late! G'night! Love ya!

Jax
> Sera!

> Damn it!

Jax stood there staring at his phone in disbelief. His sister had seen right through him. Great, he thought, there would be no hiding the fact he was interested in Charlie now. Not that he'd really intended to hide it, more that he wanted to take things slow. He didn't want to overwhelm her and she had more than enough on her plate with all the recent changes in her life. Overwhelming her might push her away. Easing into the idea of a friends-with-benefits situation was definitely the way he wanted to go.

He put his phone down and called for Chewy again as he headed toward the back door. He opened it and the dog was out the door in a flash, taking another epic flying leap into the remaining snow. Jax turned on the bright spotlight he'd installed to illuminate the yard and watched as his furry friend took care of business. His thoughts about Charlie continued to swirl and concern for her mental well-being ate away at him. Maybe he should text her?

No. No, he wasn't going to do that. She was having fun, making friends. Those were things she needed. He wasn't going to stand in her way or try to stop her from living her life – no matter how worried he was that she'd been pulled from the kiddie pool and thrown into the deep end. Lord knew his sister and friends could be quite the handful on their girls' nights. No. He was going to let her have her night and he would check in with her in the morning.

He called for Chewy and began to get ready for bed, but the overwhelming urge to check on her kept gnawing away at him. He grabbed his phone from his office and laid it on the charger on his nightstand before crawling in bed. Sleep, he thought. He'd just go to sleep. That would take that urge away. He closed his eyes and tried to relax, searching for the first floaty moments of slumber.

They didn't come.

Thirty minutes later he gave up and grabbed his phone.

> **Jax**
> Are you home yet?
>
> I hope you had a good time.
>
> Hopefully, Sera and friends weren't too wild for you.

There, he thought, that lets her know I'm thinking about her, concerned for her well-being, and hoping she enjoyed herself. Good enough. He put his phone back on the charger and tried again to go to sleep. When he found himself lying there with his mind swirling again, he slapped a hand on his face in frustration.

He flopped onto his stomach to try a different sleeping position. Maybe that would help. When his phone buzzed with a text message, he jumped and grabbed for the phone, fumbling in his efforts to get to it quickly.

The disappointment he felt when he pulled up his messages only to discover the text had come from Ryder made him roll his eyes.

> **Ryder**
> Wow! Did you see Charlie?

> **That woman is hot!**
>
> **I'm so glad Sera sent me that pic!**

Jax felt his annoyance begin to rise at the bait Ryder was dangling in front of his face. He should have known Sera would send the photo to Ryder. And now that he thought about it, Logan probably received a text of it, too. He just hadn't gotten past the way Charlie looked all dressed up for a night out to get his brain working along those lines.

He wasn't going to respond. He wasn't going to respond. Nope! Not doing it.

His resolve lasted all of thirty seconds.

Jax
> **Fuck off, Ry!**

Ryder
> **What?**
>
> **I'm just pointing out she is sexy as hell!**
>
> **Are you going to hit that?**

Jax
> **Fuck all the way off.**

Ryder

> **That's what I thought.**
>
> **No worries. I'll let you have her.**

Jax
> **Go away. Go very far away.**

Ryder
> **Awe! Love you too big guy!**

Jax
> **Fucker.**

Annoyed and frustrated, he flopped back on the bed and stared at the ceiling. When his phone signaled again, he didn't immediately pick it up. He really didn't feel like dealing with any more of Ryder's teasing. A few moments passed before he decided to look at the message. When he saw it was from Charlie, his heart skipped a beat and a huge grin quickly spread across his face.

Charlie
> **I just got home.**
>
> **I had an amazing time and way too much alcohol.**
>
> **Thanks for checking on me.**
>
> **I'll talk to you soon.**

Jax read her message three times before he was satisfied he hadn't missed anything. With a smile on his face, he put the phone back on the charger and closed his eyes. When he did, the vision of Charlie in her barely there dress floated behind his eyelids.

With a heavy sigh, he whispered a long, drawn-out "fu- uuuck." Ryder was right. She did look sexy as hell – so sexy all he could think of was getting his hands on her body and tracing her curves.

The way she piled her hair on top of her head and left her neckline bare made him want to grab her and slowly lick from the hollow of her throat up to her ear in a long, teasing line. Her skin, God, he thought, her skin was like porcelain. It wouldn't take much to mark her, to make it known she was with someone. The urge to do just that overwhelmed even as it excited him. The barely there dress she wore was designed to make your mouth water and he could all but feel the drool pooling. The cutouts of the dress played peekaboo with her stomach, the deep cut of the neckline put her cleavage on display, and the short hem of the dress made her legs appear to go on for miles.

The images began to make him throb, his cock growing and hardening. His body began to tingle and yearn as he thought of all he wanted to do to her. Her skin, he thought, would be so silky, soft, and smooth, especially the sides of her breasts. He wanted to caress her there, to cup her breasts in his hands and tease her nipples. He wanted to trail his fingers along her stomach, to feel her hips between his hands. He wanted to slowly kiss up the insides of her thighs until he reached her apex and then he wanted to bury his face in her pussy and lap up her sweetness. And, oh how sweet she would be!

Most of all, he wanted to bury his cock deep inside her, to take her virginity, to fill her up, and give her orgasm after orgasm as he pleasured them both. He wanted to take her higher than she'd ever taken herself and when they were done, he wanted to curl his large body around her and hold on. He wanted to offer warmth and comfort to her that she had so desperately lacked in her life.

The images pushed him too far. Thinking of all the amazing things they could do together, he wrapped his hands around his cock and began to work himself. He knew it wasn't going to take much to get him there, and when he felt his orgasm building at the base of his balls, his sack tightening, the tip tingling, and his shaft beginning to harden even more, he threw his head back and moaned loudly. The explosion rocked his world and his cum painted the skin of his broad chest in pearly white streams. His hand worked until he could no longer stand the heightened pleasure, and when he came down, he lay there in ecstasy. His chest heaved as he floated on ebbing waves of pleasure.

When his euphoria finally passed, he cleaned himself up and crawled back into bed. He stretched out on his stomach, a satisfied smile etched on his face, and closed his eyes.

Sleep claimed him instantly.

Charlie's head throbbed. The searing pain pulsed in a staccato bass drum beat and she could barely open her eyes. Her mouth was as dry as the Sahara and her stomach roiled with unease.

She knew she needed to get out of bed, but couldn't seem to make her muscles cooperate. In truth, she was afraid if she moved the least bit she would throw up every last drop of the margaritas she'd consumed the night before. How many had it been again? Three? No. It had been more than that, but she simply couldn't remember anything after the third one except flashes of dancing and laughing with her new friends. Shots. Had she done shots of tequila?

A shower. Maybe a shower would help her feel better, provided she could stand there long enough to take one. Gingerly, she raised her head and began the difficult process of making her muscles cooperate. When she at last found herself sitting upright on the edge of the bed, she blinked slowly and deliberately as she tried to clear the cobwebs from her mind. Her head felt as if it weighed three tons and her bedroom started to spin slowly, tilting on an axis.

Her stomach lurched, but she managed to hold back her bile and tamp down her nausea by taking a few deep breaths. She was just about to stand and make her way to the bathroom when a loud knock sounded on her door.

Oh, great, she thought. Who the heck was knocking on her door at the unholy hour of... she glanced at the bedside clock... What the? No way was it 11 am? Half the day was gone!

The knocking pattern came again and she forced herself to get up and go to the door, stumbling as she went. When the impatient knock came again, she groaned, "I'm coming. I'm coming. Don't knock so loudly!" At last, she reached the door, unlocked it, and swung it wide open. Jax stood on her doorstep, a bag in hand and Chewy at his side. For a moment all she could do was stare.

"Ah, I see. Just as I thought. Don't worry. I've come with hangover provisions." The sympathetic smile he wore was slightly ruined by the amusement that tipped up the corners of his mouth in a knowing smirk. He started to say something else but didn't get the chance. With a final lurch, her stomach revolted at last.

After her initial purge, Jax scooped her up and hurried to the bathroom. She immediately hugged the toilet bowl and continued to empty the contents of her stomach. Now, he sat beside her as she lay with her cheek on the chilly tiles of the bathroom floor and held a cool cloth to her forehead. Gently, he wiped the clammy sweat from her face and offered comforting words.

"You're going to be alright, Charlie. I promise."

"No. No, I'm not. This is awful. I'm so embarrassed!" Tears and snot began to flow uncontrollably. "Oh, my God! I threw up on you!" The tears came harder. Soon, her words became distorted and unintelligible – he couldn't make out for sure just what she was saying. Still, he offered comfort.

"Charlie. I promise you, you're going to recover. I have a few tips and tricks and I brought the BEST hangover remedy with me."

"You did?" She looked up at him pitifully.

"I did. I've used it. Logan and Ryder have used it. Hell, even the girls have used it. It works and I'm going to make sure that it works for you, too."

"Really? You're sure it will work?"

"I am. Now, why don't you take a shower, get yourself dressed, and then we'll get started."

She wiped at her tears and snuffled. "Alright." He handed her the washcloth and stood to walk to the bathroom door. "Jax?"

"Yeah?"

"Thank you. I'm so sorry I ruined your coat. And your boots."

"Nothing that a little cleaning up and a cycle in the washing machine can't fix. Don't worry about it." Once more he smiled at her. "I've got you, Little Rabbit."

Once he heard the shower running, he went to the laundry room. His coat had taken the brunt of the mess so he started there. Next, he tackled his boots and then made his way to the front door, blessing his sister as he went for not putting carpet in the entryway of the apartment.

Considering the volume Charlie had hurled, the clean-up went surprisingly quickly.

When he heard the shower cut off, he grabbed his bag of magic tricks and began lining them up on the kitchen counter. Then he loaded a plate with provisions and placed it in the microwave. Charlie entered the kitchen wearing a white silk bathrobe and slippers, her hair wrapped in a towel, at the exact moment the microwave beeped. Her face showed no signs of leftover makeup - no mascara trails or dark circles under her eyes. Though you could still see the effects of her night out, she looked somewhat refreshed and much more ready to face the day.

"There you are." Jax looked her up and down appreciatively.

"I'm so sorry you had to see me like that. I've never had a night like last night before. I've never drank that much at one time before."

"Oh, I already had that figured out."

"Okay. So what's all this?"

"This is the hangover toolkit. We have aspirin for the headache, water to hydrate, a pack of electrolytes to add to the water – a little boost for your body, and best of all," he turned to the microwave and pulled out the plate, "the best meal for getting your stomach sorted out. Today you will be starting your day with super salty french fries and a thick, juicy cheeseburger. And before you tell me there's no way you can eat that, just trust me, okay?"

He watched as her face turned a slight shade of green with the thought of adding anything to her stomach. Then he saw the transformation as her steely resolve kicked in and she nodded her head, determined to try his remedy.

"Alright. I've trusted you so far and you haven't steered me wrong yet."

He stepped to her and placed his palm on her smooth skin, cupping her cheek as he stared down into her sparkling blue eyes. "I promise not to steer you wrong, Little Rabbit – not with anything that comes along." Seeing the acceptance in her eyes, he leaned down and placed a tender kiss on her forehead.

"Feeling any better?"

Charlie was pleasantly surprised Jax's hangover toolkit had worked. She wasn't quite herself yet but considerably improved from the miserable state in which she'd woken.

"Actually, yes. I'm curious, though, how exactly did you figure all this out?"

Jax threw his head back and laughed. "Trial and error. Many, many trials and errors."

"Well, that sounds like you have stories to tell."

"Yeah. You can say that." Charlie rested her head on the back of the sofa and listened intently. "The first time I ever got hungover I was in high school. We used to go camping pretty often, me, Logan, and Ryder. The summer before our senior year we thought we knew it all. Dumb teenagers, seventeen and eighteen. Invincible. I'm pretty sure it was a mutual idea, but somewhere in our planning for the trip, we decided to raid our parents' liquor cabinets. We figured if each of us brought a little bit it wouldn't be as noticeable as if one of us tried to supply it all.

"By the time we reached our campsite, we'd already shared part of a six-pack of beer. We got everything set up – tents, campfire, the works. We were going to stay up all night, get drunk, talk about girls, brag about how much pus—... uh, how much sex we were having. You know, typical teenage boy shit. We unloaded our backpacks, lined up all the spoils we'd brought with us, and dove in.

"We were shit-faced before it was even dark. But, being the know-it-all manly men we thought we were, we kept drinking long after we should have stopped. I remember throwing up and then like a dumbass, going back for more. It's a wonder we were able to hike back down the trail the next morning. I remember the walk back taking twice as long as it did going up. There was a lot of moaning and groaning. But, we learned a valuable lesson."

"And what lesson was that?"

"Actually, we learned several lessons, but the one that pertains here is there are rules when you're drinking. One – never mix alcohol. Trust me, it's bad. Two – know your limits. Three – always make sure you've eaten before you indulge. Four – be prepared for the morning after depending on how well you follow rules one through three. We picked up a few more lessons through the years, but that's where it started."

"And what were some of the other lessons you learned that night?"

"Ah, yeah. I'm not sure you're ready to hear those lessons just yet."

"What? Why?"

"Because those lessons revolve around sex, and teenage boys and their ideas about sex."

"Oh. Well, I don't want to make you feel uncomfortable talking about it."

"I didn't say I was uncomfortable. I just don't want to offend your sensitive ears."

Charlie gasped, "My... I do not have sensitive ears!"

"Alright, let me rephrase that. Your virgin ears."

Her face flushed bright red. "Oh. Well, just because I'm a virgin doesn't mean I don't know things."

"Uh-huh."

"What? I do. I know all manner of things."

Jax couldn't help but grin at her disdain. "I'll keep that in mind. For now, I need to get back home and get some work done. Are you feeling well enough to retrieve your car? If so, you can come with me and drive it back into town."

"Goodness! I'd forgotten about the car! Umm, yeah. I'll get some clothes on and ride up with you."

"Alright."

She rose from the sofa and walked toward the bedroom. When Jax grabbed her hand and stopped her in her tracks, she looked down at him in confusion.

"For the record, I was rather enjoying the sight of you sitting here in your robe." His eyes roamed up and down her body, lingering on her breasts.

Once again a blush crept up her neck and across her cheeks. "Oh. Well, I, uh..."

He rubbed his thumb back and forth across the back of her hand, a tender caress, suggestive and telling of his intentions. She stared into his eyes and what she saw there made her breath hitch. She'd never experienced true desire before but had read about it in so many books through the years that she knew, without a doubt, that was what she was seeing in his gaze.

He smiled up at her, "Another time, Little Rabbit. Another time."

Chapter Ten

Charlie's phone rang loudly and abruptly pulled her from the depths of the book she was reading. Though she was loathe to return to the land of the living from the make-believe world of magic, dragons, fairy princesses, and romantic encounters, she reached for the phone and looked at the readout. When she saw Jax's name pop on the screen, she smiled and answered, anticipation lightly tripping in her chest.

"Hello, Jaxon."

"Have dinner with me."

"You could say hello."

"I could. Hello, Charlotte Grace. Have dinner with me."

She laughed, "Well, that's better, at least."

"Charlie. It's been a week since I've found time to come up for air from the project I'm working on. It has been a week since you've been treated to my effortless charm and witty sarcasm. It has been a week since I've stared into your gorgeous eyes. Have dinner with me. Tonight. Please?"

"Alright." She grinned and bit her lip as giddiness made her heart skip a beat.

"I'll pick you up at seven. Wear something like you wore when you went out with the girls."

"You want me to wear something skimpy and revealing?"

"Why wouldn't I, Little Rabbit?"

"I don't know if you noticed or not, but the temperature has dropped drastically over the past two days."

"Wear a coat."

"Well, obviously I'll need a coat."

"Charlie..." His voice deepened drastically and sent shivers up and down her spine.

"Yes, Jax?"

"I promise to keep you warm..." The sudden change in the tone of his voice sent a tingling current straight down her spine. Charlie squeezed her legs together as liquid desire swamped her and threatened to drown her in need.

"Oh... Uh... Okay."

"And Charlie?"

"Yes?"

"No getting drunk tonight. I don't want anything to mess with your memory of our time together. I'll see you later."

When the call ended, Charlie lowered the phone from her ear and stared at it as if it were a foreign object. What, she wondered, just happened? From the moment they met, Jax had been friendly and caring. At times he'd even been sweet, but he'd never shown more than mild flirtation. That, she thought, was so much more than mild flirtation. That...well, that had been blatantly sexual.

The idea that a man like Jax might be interested in her sexually thrilled her to no end. Being wanted in any capacity at all was a new experience for her. Being wanted sexually? Well, that just made her want to giggle like a schoolgirl.

She shook her head to clear it of the images that suddenly popped into her mind then picked up her book to get back to her story. When she found herself reading the same paragraph for the fifth time, she gave up. She glanced at the clock and even though it was way too early to start getting ready for her night out, she couldn't help herself.

She hurried to the bathroom and began to strip out of her clothes. When she caught her reflection in the mirror out of the corner of her eye, she had to look twice. She almost didn't recognize herself. She turned then and stared at herself straight on, studying her features. She looked like she always did with one major exception.

A beautiful smile lit her face and she radiated happiness from within.

"Why, Charlotte Grace! Could it be? Could you have found where you belong? Are you truly happy for the first time in your life?"

She gently bit her bottom lip as her smile spread further than ever. Then she hugged herself as she turned a circle gleefully.

As she stepped into the shower, she began to sing loudly and off-key. Life, she thought, was finally getting good!

Jax opened the door to Ryder's house and let Chewy run inside ahead of him. When he heard the "oof" of breath being knocked out of Ryder as Chewy landed on him, he grinned from ear to ear and shut the door behind him.

"Damn it, Jax! Teach your son some manners!"

"He has manners! He thinks of you as family, Ry!"

"Yeah, well, family usually sits on the sofa itself, not on top of the sofa's occupants."

"Whatever. Thanks for watching him for me tonight, man."

"Always willing to do my part in helping a friend get laid."

"Dude!"

"Don't dude me. You know as well as I do what your end game is here."

"True. Just, have a little class, alright? She's a classy lady. You don't need to be so crass when you're talking about her."

"Fine. Whatever. You're taking your new lady friend out for a classy dinner at a classy restaurant. That's very classy of you, Jax."

"See? That wasn't so hard, now, was it?"

"Of course not! I just hope for her sake that when y'all actually fuck you lose some of that class. It'll be a whole hell of a lot more fun for both of you."

"Asshole!"

"Assholery is what I do best."

"Just...take care of my dog."

"You sure he isn't a bear? I really think he's a bear."

"I'm leaving now."

"Yeah, yeah. Go class it up with your classy lady."

As he walked out the door, he heard Ryder fussing at Chewy to get down. Then he heard a crash and the unmistakable sound of breaking glass. Jax took tremendous pleasure from the chaos and subsequent litany of curse words flowing from his friend. It served Ryder right for insulting Charlie.

Nobody, he thought, was going to get by with treating her badly as long as he was around. He wouldn't hear of it.

When Jax pulled up to Charlie's apartment, he put his Jeep in park and turned off the engine. He sat for a moment and looked up at the lone lightbulb burning next to Charlie's apartment door – a beacon lighting his path to what he hoped was a fun night with an amazing woman.

It had been a long fucking week and he was mentally drained. The first part of the week had been dedicated to designing a new program for a long-time customer, and the remainder of the week putting out metaphorical fires for two other customers. The longer the week had droned on, the slower the days had passed for him. Looking back he could now see part of that reason had been the fact that he couldn't get Charlie out of his mind.

It didn't seem to matter what he was doing, she was constantly in his thoughts. And when he went to bed at night, those thoughts instantly turned sexual in design. He hadn't woken with the results of a wet dream in years – until this week, that is. If he didn't jerk off to mental images of her when he first laid down, it was guaranteed he would wake up covered in a mess sometime in the middle of the night. It was a bit annoying but invigorating at the same time.

He felt like a horny teenager. Part of him hated the fact that she had hijacked his thoughts, even though he thoroughly enjoyed the heightened sexual gratification. Part of him didn't mind having her perpetually floating through his mind. Who wouldn't want a beautiful, interesting, entertaining woman constantly in their thoughts? The fact that she was highly unaware of how sexy she was added to her appeal and made him want her even more.

It had been many years since he'd been infatuated with a woman. It was kind of nice for a change. It had taken him lying awake a couple of nights and thinking back over his 'one and dones' and his 'dial-a-friend when you need a friends' to make him realize he'd become complacent in his ways. He couldn't remember the last time he'd taken a woman out on a date as opposed to sending a text for a casual hookup just to scratch an itch.

He couldn't see himself doing that with Charlie. She was too innocent, too sweet, and too perfect, to ruin with that kind of treatment.

He checked his phone to see what time it was and then with a smile on his face, climbed out of his car and hurried up the three flights of stairs to knock on her door. He raised his fist to knock, but before he could even wrap his knuckles against the heavy wood, she opened the door, surprising him and making him chuckle.

"Well, hello there, Little Rabbit." He couldn't keep the grin from his face, and he couldn't keep himself from looking her over from head to toe. What he saw made his heart skip a beat and the need to kiss her tried to overpower him.

"Hello, Jaxon." She smiled as she looked up at him and stepped backward to let him inside and shut out the freezing evening air.

"You look amazing."

She looked down at the dress she wore and smoothed her hands over the shiny material. "You like it?"

"Like is not a powerful enough word for my feelings on that dress and you being in it." A rosy blush crept up her neck and into her cheeks.

"Oh, well, you can thank your sister. She left a bunch of dresses over here when we went out."

Jax winced. "Now, see, I could have gone all night without knowing you're wearing one of my sister's dresses."

Charlie laughed and as the musical sound floated through the air, it made ripples of need begin to stir within him. "Sorry. It's just, I don't own things like this. This would not be acceptable attire in my house."

"I guess we can make some concessions for tonight. But, Charlie, let me make a suggestion."

"Alright. What is your suggestion?"

"The first chance you get, go shopping. Go wild. Fill your closet with clothes you want, with clothes that fit the new you and the new life you're embracing. You deserve to do and be and live the way you truly want. You deserve to have the things you want, the clothes you want, the friends you want. Don't let your past life color your new life. Cut the cord."

"You know what? You're right. Maybe I can get the girls to come with me and we can make a day of it."

"There ya go! And speaking of going, I'm starving. Shall we?"

"Absolutely!"

Soft candlelight reflected off the teardrop crystals of the extravagant chandeliers which had been dimmed for ambiance in the intimate dining room of the restaurant. The elegance of the room was accented by ecru linens covering the tables and the dark mahogany of the wooden chairs. Champagne filled their fluted glasses and the occasional bubble rose from the bottom, a shooting star rushing to the top and popping with effervescence.

Charlie had been pleasantly surprised when they'd stepped into the foyer of the restaurant. She'd been unsure what to expect when Jax had told her he was taking her to The Gold Rush. The name, it seemed, was deceiving. Knowing her background, he had been concerned she wouldn't be impressed, but she felt certain this fine dining experience ranked up there with some of the Michelin-star restaurants she'd frequented throughout her life. What he failed to realize was it wouldn't have mattered to her if they'd done nothing more than sit in a mom-and-pop diner to share their meal. It was the experience and the company she enjoyed more than anything.

Their meals had come and gone, their banter had been lively throughout the evening, and now they lingered, splitting a piece of Black Forest Cake for dessert.

"Tell me more about leaving New England. What was it that finally pushed you, Charlie?"

"There isn't much more to tell, Jax. I reached my limit. I just couldn't live that way any longer."

"Alright. Let's play a game. I'll tell you my suspicions and you tell me if I'm hot or cold."

"Jax..."

"I've done more research, Charlotte. I know about the money problems."

"Seriously? You need to stop invading my privacy! Why can't you accept that I'm not ready to share so much of myself just yet?" The frustration she felt at his unwillingness to let her open up to him in her own time and way rang through her voice.

"I'm not doing it to be an ass. I'm doing it because I'm worried." He sighed, "I'm doing it because I care."

Suddenly no longer craving the rich chocolate cake, she placed her fork on the plate and sat back in her chair. "Just let it go, Jax. It's done."

"You know they may come looking for you. What will you do if they find you?"

"I'll run again. I don't know where I'll go, but I'll leave. I can't go back to that life. I won't. I refuse to live like that, to live through that."

"They will keep coming for you. You know that, right?"

"You obviously found out quite a bit. How far did you go? Did you discover all of our deep dark secrets?"

"I don't know if I found them all, but I found enough. It took some digging, Charlie, but once I figured out where to look and what to look for, the pattern was there. Unmistakable. The near bankruptcies. The mishandled funds. The illegitimate children, forced marriages, blackmail. It's all there if you look hard enough, close enough. Will you really run again? Why not try standing up to them?"

"I don't know what else to do. Running is all I've got." She shook her head as she considered. "Stand up to them? I don't know if I have what it takes inside me to stand up to anyone, much less my parents."

"You do. I fully believe you do."

"Thanks for that, but I have to believe it myself and I'm not there yet. In fact, I don't know if I'll ever believe it." The look on his face told her she was hitting a nerve with him. In the extremely short time she'd gotten to know him, she had already figured out he was one of those people who believed you could do anything you set your mind to do.

"I know you didn't ask me to do it, but I did what I could to help cover more of your tracks. I even put out some breadcrumbs to lead them away from you." Jax reached for her hand and took it in his as he looked deeply into her eyes. "I want to help. Let me help you."

"You already are and I appreciate all you've done for me. I can't let you get involved in this, at least not any more than what you already are. They... They aren't good people. Not like you, Logan, and Sera. Not like all the new friends I've made so quickly here. They hurt people.

They abuse the people they supposedly love with mental anguish, by forcing them into untenable situations. I don't want their sins to stain your life. I don't want you to get hurt, Jax."

"Little Rabbit. You can run. You can hide. But one of these days you're going to have to stand up to them. You're going to have to do something drastic or they will never truly let you go so you can live your life. Do you want to look over your shoulder all the time?"

"No. No, I don't." She paused and closed her eyes as she took a deep breath. When she at last raised her icy blue gaze, she pleaded with him. "Give me time, Jax. I just need time." After a moment she saw acceptance in his eyes, however tentative, and exhaled in relief.

Jax followed closely behind Charlie as she climbed the stairs to her apartment. The short drive from the restaurant had been filled with nervous tension. He could tell she was unsure what to expect as far as ending their date. And while he wanted nothing more than to grab her and cart her off to her bed to have his way with her and clear her mind of all thoughts but them and what they were making each other feel, he resisted. It was going to happen. He was determined to make it happen. But he knew slow and steady was the only race she could handle. Otherwise, his little rabbit just might get frightened away.

Charlie pulled her keys from her clutch to unlock the door and immediately began to fumble with the lock. He wasn't certain if it was cold or nerves, but he was betting on the latter. Wrapping one arm around her waist and reaching with the other, he took the chain from her and smoothly slid the key into the lock.

She looked over her shoulder and up at him and the uncertainty he saw there confirmed his suspicions. She was nervous.

"Uh, thank you." She stepped into the apartment and began to remove her coat, but Jax remained on the threshold. She looked back at him in confusion. "Aren't you coming in?"

"No. Not this time, Little Rabbit." He smiled at her as he did his best to hide just how anxious he was to do all the things she was nervous about.

Her face fell in disappointment and almost broke his resolve. "I see."

"No. No, you don't see. Which is why I'm not coming in this time, Charlie." She looked up at him, confused hopefulness written all over her face. "This time."

"So, there will be another time?"

An endearing smile crossed his face. "Come here." She stepped to him and he pulled her in for a hug. He held on to her for a few moments, offering her a moment of sanctuary in his arms. "Charlotte Grace. There will most definitely be another time. And I hope there will be more after that."

He pulled back from her and gazed into her upturned face, then he tucked a strand of hair behind her ear and trailed a fingertip down her cheek. Holding her chin in his hand, he brushed his thumb along the edge of her bottom lip. Unable to resist any longer, he leaned in and kissed her – a tender brush against her plump lips before he pulled back and searched her face for acceptance. The tiny gasp of breath that left her lungs made him want to dive in for more. He kissed her again, letting his lips linger with promises of pleasures to come. And when he pulled back again, he placed a tender kiss on her forehead and turned to go.

Halfway down the stairs, he looked back up at her and smiled. "It's cold, Charlotte. I promised to keep you warm. Go inside now. Don't make me break my promise." He watched as she grinned, nodded her head, and closed the door. Then he got in his car and started the engine, grinning as he backed out of the parking spot.

He couldn't remember the last time he felt such excited anticipation about a woman. With happiness swirling within him, he headed to Ryder's to retrieve his dog.

Chapter Eleven

Three days later, Charlie flipped through rack after rack of clothing. It hadn't taken much to convince her new friends she needed to go shopping. Sera, Alex, and Val had been excited to help her fill her closet with clothes specifically chosen for the life she was now making for herself.

They'd started the day early and had been going non-stop. Their adventures had taken them two hours south into Durango where they'd gone to every store they could find. Now, they were at their last stop before starting their return trip.

"Oh, my!" Charlie turned to where Sera stood holding a silky piece of material that appeared to be nothing more than scraps draped across a hanger. "This. You have to get this, Charlie!"

She apprehensively reached for the hanger and examined the front of the dress before turning it around and looking at the other side. But on closer inspection, she wasn't entirely sure which was which. "Oh, I don't think so."

"Yes. Absolutely."

"No..."

"Girl! Trust me! At least try it on!"

"Sera," Charlie whispered, "I can't tell what part goes where."

Sera laughed, loud and robust. "Come on. I'll help. I promise you are going to look fabulous in this!"

After spending the day with her friends and witnessing their steely determination to help her deconstruct and reconstruct her wardrobe, she knew better than to argue. When she stepped out of the dressing room and looked herself over in the three-way mirror, she knew Sera had been right. It was a fabulous dress – what there was of it. Thoughts of wearing it for Jax and what his reaction might be flashed through her mind. Giddiness surged and she couldn't keep the smile from her face.

"I told you."

"Yes. You most certainly did."

"Holy crap!" Alex and Val walked over to where they stood, offering catcalls and whistles. "Check you out! You've gone from proper debutante to sexy siren in a heartbeat!"

"I love it, but I just... I don't know. Are you sure this is all there is to it?" She turned and examined the back of it. "Is everything covered?"

"You're overthinking it! Trust us! This dress has your name written all over it!"

Charlie turned to her friends for confirmation and as each head nodded their agreement, she couldn't help but grin. She was having the best time and she couldn't wait to get home and hang all her new clothes in her closet. She couldn't wait to throw away some of the clothes her mother had considered appropriate attire for someone of her position in society. Most of all, she couldn't wait to wear some of her new items the next time she was around Jax – the dress she currently wore topping the list.

"Well, ladies. Are we done here? I'm starving and am desperate for a drink!"

"Alex. You're always desperate for a drink."

"True. Since you know this, why are you torturing me?"

"Alright, alright! Charlie, go change. Toss that dress and the rest of your stack out here to me and I'll head to the checkout."

Charlie opened her mouth to object but was cut off before she could. "Nope." Alex raised her hand to halt her objections and shook her head. "No arguing. This time it's our treat."

"But I..."

"Charlie. You might as well just let us do what we want." Val looked to Sera and Alex for confirmation. "We're going to do it anyway. This is our little welcome to you."

"Thank you all. I," tears threatened to fall and she found herself choking up at the thought of finally having friends, "don't know how I got so lucky as to find all of you, but I'm so glad I did!"

"You belong here. You belong with us. You belong in Ouray. Now hurry up! Drinks are waiting!"

The drive back to Ouray seemed to fly by. Laughter flowed as stories were told. They had decided to go home for dinner instead of eating in Durango so they could all get as drunk as they wanted and not have to worry about driving.

By the time they reached Logan's bar, they were a little loud, a little rowdy, and more than ready to get their drinks on. Their conversation never stopped as they hurried from the car into the warmth of the bar and began removing their coats.

"Alright. So, how exactly are you this old and haven't gotten nasty with someone yet? You're sexy as hell, Charlie!"

"Alex!" Sera and Val both admonished their friend.

"No. No, it's alright. I've just never been interested in anyone that way. Back home nobody ever noticed whether I was around or not. And I was a master at hiding in plain sight. I didn't want anyone to notice me – at least not any of the people I was forced to associate with. The one guy I had a bit of a crush on as a teenager never really seemed to pay any attention to whether I was there or not. I was invisible to him and to almost everyone else."

"There's quite a bit you aren't telling us, isn't there, Charlie?" Sera looked at her with concern.

"There's a lot I can't tell you. At least, not yet, I can't."

"Well, you can tell us about this guy. Why didn't he notice you? Why didn't you let him see you, the real you?"

"Yeah, see...that gets into things I can't talk about. What I can tell you is that he didn't mind one bit when I stopped trying to talk to him. I guess I was an annoyance."

"Men!" Val shook her head in disgust.

"Now Val... You're the only one of us who is happily married."

"You'll be soon enough, bitch. Logan would run to the courthouse in a heartbeat if you would agree to it.

He's indulging you and your romantic nature with all the wedding planning. And, just because I'm married doesn't mean it is always happy. We've had our hard times. In fact, we're having one of those rough times right now. Sometimes I wonder what he would do if I took the kids and left. If I just called it quits. There are times I know he would go crazy without us and there are times I don't think he would mind at all if we were gone. Well, he would miss the kids, but I'm not so sure he would miss me. It is a horrible feeling knowing you love and are committed to someone who might not blink an eye at the thought of you being gone."

"Here is my advice and you can take it or leave it, Val. Don't lose your mind over someone who doesn't mind losing you."

"You're so cynical, Alex." Sera shook her head.

"Yeah, well, if you had ever had your heart ripped from your body, stomped on, and left in a million pieces, you would understand." Alex walked away in a huff and left her friends standing there, angrily punching her way through the swinging doors of the bar as she went. They watched as their friend headed straight to the bathroom, ignoring the people in the crowd who called out to her as she passed.

"Do either of you want to tell me what that was all about?" Charlie looked back and forth between Sera and Val for an explanation.

"It's Alex's story to tell, but I warn you that she won't talk about it easily, if at all. She had a bad experience when she was a teenager and she's shunned all relationships since then. She prefers casual sex and friends with benefits. I don't think she will ever willingly get into a relationship again."

"I'm going to go out on a limb here and say that it has something to do with the animosity she exhibits toward Ryder."

"You, Charlie, are an intuitive person. The thing is," Val looked at Sera for confirmation, "if the two of them would actually sit down and have a conversation it might clear the air and would make all of our lives easier. But no. Instead the two of them have to be the most stubborn people on the face of the planet."

"Should we go after her?"

"Nah, she's alright – let's go get a table." Sera began walking toward the back of the bar, talking over her shoulder as she went. "She just has to get it out of her system then she'll be fine. Or, she'll be fine until the next time she has a run-in with Ryder."

"This is all so intriguing! It's just like a story from one of your books, Sera!"

"With the exception of the fact that if it was a story from one of my books I could make these two talk to each other. With Alex and Ryder? It's a crap shoot as to whether it will ever happen or not and the dice are heavily loaded toward not."

A drinking song poured from the speakers as they gathered around their table and gave their orders to a passing waitress. "Well I, for one, want to hear more about you and Jax. When's the big day?"

"What do you mean by 'big day,' Val?" Charlie looked at her in confusion.

"Really? You are not that dense. Naive, maybe, but not dense."

"What Val is trying to ask is, when are you and my brother going to get busy so that all these sexual vibes stop buzzing all around us? There's only so much swatting we can do before they drive us insane."

"Oh." Charlie giggled. "I don't know. He's so sweet and patient. I think he thinks I need easing into it when in reality I just want him to grab me and... well, you know."

"Yes. Yes, we know!" All three of them began to laugh heartily.

Logan suddenly appeared at their table and set their first round of drinks in front of them. "Now what is it that has the three of you in such a good mood?"

Sera smiled up at her fiance. "Oh, you know. We're just talking about sex."

Logan wiggled an eyebrow at Sera and touched his tongue to his top lip as he considered, "Well that's certainly a subject that puts me in a good mood."

Sera narrowed her eyes as she flirted back at him, "Kiss me and then get back behind that bar before you get in trouble with your boss."

"Funny." Logan placed his hands on either side of her face and sealed her lips with his own, pouring himself into it. Sera's body visibly began to liquefy with lust. When he pulled back, she was breathless and bleary-eyed with a sexual haze. Then he kissed her forehead tenderly and walked to the bar. Charlie watched the interaction in fascination.

"Talk about buzzing vibes. Buzz. Buzz."

"I'll say. That was so hot, Sera! The way he looks at you makes me swoon. I wonder..." she stopped and looked wistfully into the deep bowl of her margarita, "I wonder if Jax will ever look at me that way?"

Sera and Val stared at her, incredulous that she didn't see what they saw. "Charlie, honey. He's been looking at you like that all along. You haven't noticed?"

"Well, no. I mean...I know he wants me. I can tell that easily enough. But he's not in love with me." She stopped and thought back over every moment she'd shared with Jax since her arrival. She just didn't see it. "He's not, right? In love with me?"

"Oh, do we ever have our work cut out for us!"

"Do you want to start, Sera, or should I? Should we wait for Alex?"

"Nah. She'll catch up. By all means, Val, take the lead. I'm just going to sit here and get a little drunk while we discuss my brother's love life."

"Alright, Charlie. It's like this..."

Jax hadn't expected to see Charlie when he decided to come out of hiding and have a drink with his friends. When he'd finally surfaced from work that afternoon, it had been with an antsy feeling – an urge for something he couldn't quite place his finger on. A quick text to Ryder and plans had been made to invade Logan's bar and get a little drunk.

Then he'd walked through the swinging doors of the bar and seen her sitting with his sister and friends. All thoughts of enjoying a night with Logan and Ryder flew out the window in a heartbeat. Now, all he wanted to do was grab her, throw her over his shoulder, and go find somewhere quiet to begin a slow seduction that would lead to a ravishing first experience.

He wasn't sure how he'd managed to control himself and merely wave at the table full of beautiful women before going through the pass-through of the shiny mahogany bar and helping himself to a beer. He couldn't take his eyes off Charlie as he pulled the tap and filled his mug. And as he topped off his glass, the realization that she'd gotten under his skin finally began to sink in. Part of him began to silently scream denials while the other part of him began to beg for mercy.

"Don't do it." Ryder walked behind the bar and helped himself just as Jax had.

"Don't do what?"

Logan looked to where his friends stood talking and laughed. "He's saying don't disturb girls' night. But what he really means is, don't fall for her."

"Bingo." Ryder pointed a finger at Logan and nodded his head in agreement.

"Who said I was going to do either of those things?"

"He doesn't see it, does he?" Ryder glanced at Logan for confirmation.

"Nope." Logan shook his head.

"See what?"

"You're falling for her and you're falling hard."

Panic began to beat a steady pulse through his body. Was it that obvious?

"Oh geez. Don't tell him that shit, Logan! Just because you're a lovesick fool doesn't mean he has to follow you down the rabbit hole of insanity. Stay with me here, Jax. Stay on the path of endless nookie from multiple pussies. We're good over here. They know us here. You're safe here. If you latch onto her, you'll be lost in the monotony of monogamy. Don't you want to stay where there's a bevy of beavers? You know you love to DoorDash some ass."

Logan threw the towel he'd been wiping down the bar with at Ryder. "Cynical asshole!"

"Cynicism is healthy. It keeps me sane."

"Will the two of you stop?" Jax took a long, slow drink of his beer as he contemplated. He swallowed and felt the ice-cold liquid claw its way down his throat as the reality of what he was feeling for Charlie began to burn through him with clear certainty.

"Oh, God. There it is. That's the look. Son of a bitch. I've lost both of you now, haven't I? Fuck!" Ryder turned up his beer and chugged until his mug was dry.

Jax sat his half-empty mug on the bar top and with a determined look on his face walked over to where the table full of beautiful women sat having dinner and enjoying themselves.

"Ladies."

A chorus of, "Hey, Jax!" echoed around the table.

Leaning down to eye-level with Charlie, Jax gazed intently into her icy blue eyes while offering her his hand. "May I borrow you for a minute?"

Charlie's heart beat rapidly. The look Jax was giving her made her tingle from head to toe. Panic began to set in. From what her new friends told her, Jax was smitten with her. From the look on his face at the moment, she was prone to believe them. She couldn't understand exactly why, but she was definitely beginning to think they were correct.

Unsure what to do, she looked quickly at her new friends for guidance. Sera sat with her hands clasped in glee. Alex smirked, a smug look on her face, and Val nodded her head in encouragement.

She turned back to Jax and tentatively placed her hand in his, rising from her seat as she did. Hand in hand Jax led her away from her friends, down the back hallway, and toward the restrooms. Oh, God, she thought. Surely he isn't going to ask me to have sex with him in the restroom! She wanted something special for her first time. She wanted a bed. She wanted candlelight. She wanted music. She wanted more than a rushed experience in a public restroom!

When Jax opened the door to a storage room instead, she stepped inside and hoped she didn't make a fool of herself. She was barely in the room before Jax grabbed her from behind and wrapped his arms around her, pressing his body close.

"Charlie..." His frenzied whisper sent an icy thrill down her spine.

With one arm wrapped tightly around her waist, he anchored her body next to his. With his other hand, he slid the long strands of her hair off her neck and out of the way. When she felt his hot breath as his lips lingered a hair's breadth from touching her skin, she felt her knees go weak. Once again, he whispered her name and when he did, she felt a surge of hot liquid begin to pool in the front of her lacy thong.

Her brain short-circuited. She didn't know what she was supposed to do. She tried to think like one of her favorite book heroines to see if she could pull off some amount of confidence in her actions and reactions, but nothing but a blank appeared where her thoughts usually floated.

When his lips finally touched her skin, tenderly kissing the softness of her neck, an internal knowledge kicked into gear. Suddenly she didn't have to think. She knew what to do and she wasted no time in acting on her newly discovered knowledge.

She let her head fall back against his shoulder and gloried in the sensations of his perfect lips as they tasted and teased. She moaned as she reached up and behind her to tangle her fingers in his thick hair, pulling him closer without even realizing she was doing it. A loud moan echoed throughout the small room and when she realized that sound had come from deep within her own chest, she could hardly believe her ears.

Had that really been her? That sexy, seductive moan? Oh, God!

Before she knew it, Jax turned her and quickly guided her back against the storage room door, pushing up against her and trapping her body with his. Her breathing ragged, she looked up at him expectantly. Suddenly, his mouth crashed down on hers and she swore her heart would beat out of her chest. Hunger. She'd never experienced a hunger like this before. She wanted him. She wanted her first experience to be with this sweet, caring, amazing man. And as much as she hated the thought of her first time being somewhere as unappealing as a storage room, she wanted that first experience now.

Chapter Twelve

Jax swore there was steam coming out of his ears. Something had clicked inside him as he talked with Logan and Ryder. It was as if a sign had been given and it was flashing neon at him. Somehow, in that moment, he knew, Charlie was it for him. They hardly knew each other but without a doubt he believed they belonged together. Interrupting her girls' night hadn't been in the plan for the evening, but he couldn't bear the thought of not tasting her – not when he'd just had the epiphany that they were meant to be.

Now he wasn't sure if he could stop. A kiss. Though he wanted more, all he needed was a kiss. It was all he'd intended from the moment he'd walked from behind the bar. Something to sate his hunger until he could plan a special evening with her. But when her moan had built from the pit of her stomach and slowly rolled up through her body, he'd heard and felt it rise within and it was all he could do to keep from pulling her to the floor and having his way with her.

He didn't want that for their first time together, and he most certainly didn't want that for her first time ever. With her pressed against the door and their mouths and tongues seeking and finding, giving and taking, he knew he was going to have to be the one to stop them before they went too far. She was just as lost in the moment as he was.

But first, he needed more. Just a bit more, he thought as his tongue tangled with hers. A bit more of her lips. A bit more of her tongue. A bit more of her fruity breath filling his lungs as they tasted and teased.

He was hard – rock solid – and his cock throbbed with want and need. Her hands tentatively began to roam up his chest, exploring his body. Suddenly, she began to get bolder and her hands slid around his waist to his back, gently massaging and kneading. His heart pounded as he relished the feel of her hands on him. He couldn't remember the last time he was this turned on. The sensations hit hard, overwhelming him almost immediately. When the tingling began in his balls, he knew he was a goner. Boldly, her hands slid down and gripped his ass. When she squeezed each cheek, he lost it.

He felt the surge as his cum began to spurt out of him, a skyrocket that blew his mind at the same time it filled his boxer briefs. He gasped as he broke their kiss and threw his head back, giving in to bliss. His chest heaved as he savored the moment. It never even occurred to him to be embarrassed by his lack of control. Instead, he simply enjoyed the rush of adrenaline and euphoria that flowed like a river throughout his body.

When at last he felt himself coming back down from his orgasmic high, he glanced down expecting to see Charlie with the same sexual haze covering her eyes. What he saw instead made alarm bells begin to blare in his mind. Wide-eyed with uncertainty and her face pale, Charlie stood, stiff as a board with panic and confusion written on every feature. Jax knew immediately he'd gone too far too fast.

His mind began to whirl with how to handle the situation.

"I..."

"Charlie..." Jax tenderly placed his hands on either side of her face, cupping her cheeks, and guided her eyes to his. "You're amazing."

"I...I am?"

He placed a sweet kiss on her lips and then her forehead. "I've never met a woman like you. I've never wanted another woman the way I want you. I've never needed another woman the way I need you."

"But...did what I think happened really just happen?"

He chuckled, "Yeah. Yeah, it did."

"But I... But we..." Charlie continued to fumble over her words and as she did, Jax found it incredibly endearing. The wordsmith before him, the linguaphile, was at a loss for words. Something about that made him want to preen. Hell, he thought, all we've done is kiss. What's she going to do when we take it a step further?

Charlie was astounded. "What did I do wrong?"

"Nothing. You did nothing wrong. Oh, Little Rabbit, you did everything right. In fact, you did it a little too right. Everything about you is a little too right."

"I hardly touched you. I don't understand."

"That's right. You did hardly touch me. Think about that for a minute, Charlie. You barely touched me and made that happen. That should do wonderfully amazing things to your ego."

She could hardly believe what she was hearing. She had made him orgasm. She'd hardly done anything and it had happened. It had been fast. It had been intense. It had been unbelievably stimulating. Even now there was a wetness between her legs that was proof of just how much she wanted the sexy man who stood before her, and that wetness had only grown when he'd first begun to climax.

"Well, I..."

"Shhh..." He placed a finger against her lips to silence her. "I brought you back here because I wanted a moment alone with you. I wanted to kiss you. Really kiss you, for the first time. I didn't intend for it to go that far.

She nodded her head in understanding as she listened to him. "Basorexia."

"Baso... what?"

"Basorexia. It is an irresistible desire or strong urge to kiss someone. That's what you had and I guess I did, too."

"You're incredible. I don't know how you keep all that information inside your head, but you're simply incredible."

She found herself smiling uncontrollably. "I've always had that ability. Once I read something, it stays with me. I've never been tested, but I suspect I have a photographic memory."

"Fascinating. Absolutely fascinating. Charlie. In case you haven't noticed, I'm highly attracted to you. I feel like I know quite a bit about you, but I want to know more. I want to know everything."

"I feel the same about you, Jaxon."

"The day after tomorrow, Charlie – Friday. Let's plan an evening together on Friday and see where it takes us. What do you say?"

"I would love that."

Charlie slid into her seat at the table and picked up the remains of her margarita. As she watched Jax grab his coat from the coat closet and walk out the door, she guzzled the fruity liquid and emptied the glass.

"I think it's safe to say someone got some action. Give us the deets!"

"Alex! Give her a moment to catch her breath!" Giggles went up around the table.

"That was... I, umm, I don't have the words," a quizzical look crossed her face, "which is weird because I always have words, for how..."

"Hot?"

"Sexy?"

"Arousing?" Sera raised an eyebrow in question.

"That. That's the word. See? There's a reason you're the author."

"Well, then! Fill us in!"

"Alex. I swear." Val shook her head.

"No. It's alright. I, well, you all know I've never had girlfriends before. Now that I do – I can consider you all my girlfriends, right?"

"Oh, sweetheart. Of course, you can! You're one of the girls now. And while we haven't known you long, I can guarantee you a slot as a best friend. You belong with us. You belong in Ouray. You, my dear, belong with Jax."

"Yes! Back to the good stuff!"

"Lordy! You better fill us in before Alex pops a blood vessel."

"Alright. He took me back there to the storage room. I panicked. I thought he was going to take me into a restroom. I thought he wanted to, well...you know."

"We know." All three friends spoke at once and again, giggles floated on the airwaves.

"But, he didn't. We didn't. Well, we sort of didn't."

"Whoa... Maybe you better explain the 'sort of didn't' " Sera picked up her margarita and downed the last of it.

"We walked into the storage room and the next thing I knew he had my back against the door, caging me in and kissing the hell out of me. It was the most provocative and thrilling moment of my life."

"Hell, yeah! Go Jax!" Alex put both hands in the air, palms out in a praise form.

"Fuck. For a minute there I forgot we were talking about my brother. I'm going to have to have another drink to handle this."

"It was fabulous. I'll never forget it. I do have a question, though. And you guys are all experienced, so you'll be able to tell me if what happened is...unusual."

"Oh, hell. It was just kissing, right? There's no way he screwed that up."

"Well, we were really into it. I was freaked out at first, but I really got into it. Like, really, really into it. So, I touched him."

"Oh, honey. Was it your first time touching a dick?"

Val rolled her eyes, "Alright. You're cut off. No more alcohol for you tonight, Alex."

"I didn't. I swear. I just hugged him and ran my hands up and down his back. And when I did, he became more aroused. I was kind of lost in the moment and without even thinking about it, I... Holy crap! I grabbed his butt!"

"Ass. You grabbed his ass. Come on, honey. Work with us here." Alex looked at her pleadingly.

"Alright," Val nodded her head. "You grabbed his ass. No big deal. Jax has a great ass."

"Oh, he really does, doesn't he?" Charlie smiled dreamily.

"God damn it! Why am I listening to stories about my brother's sex life and body?"

"Hush! Let her finish. I think we're getting to the good part." Alex looked at Charlie for confirmation.

"Yes. Well, something happened when I grabbed his bu... ass. He...Oh, my God. He...he orgasmed." Everyone began speaking at once.

"What the hell?"

"No fucking way!"

"I'm not hearing this! I'm not hearing this!"

"Yep! He did it right in his blue jeans. I freaked out. I must have done something wrong, right? But Jaxon, he was amazing. He told me I had done everything right."

"Well, yes, honey. Orgasms are what we want our sexual encounters to culminate in. So you definitely did something right. Jax, however, better get a grip – ha ha! See what I did there?"

"Yes, Alex. We all see." Val shook her head at her friend. "Girl. Take that as a feather in your cap. This man wants you and is so turned on by you and your touch that he couldn't hold back. That is so damn special!"

"It is?" Charlie thought for a moment and then a mischievous smile spread across her face. "You're right. It is special."

"It is also the reason he cut his night short. I'm sure he didn't want to be walking around here with all that mess in his jeans." Alex snickered as she picked up her margarita and took a big gulp.

"Good Lord! That's it. I'm going to the bar and begging my fiance for a shot or two. I can't take this without substantially more alcohol."

They watched as Sera hurried to the bar and up to Logan. When they saw her begin to talk rapidly, her hands flying as she spoke, and Logan grabbing a shot glass, they began to laugh.

"Well, then. What's next Ms. Magic Hands?" Val leaned back in her chair and grinned from ear to ear.

"We're getting together Friday night. At my place. He's coming to my place and we're maybe going to... Wow. I may lose my virginity Friday night!"

"I can guarantee you if you wear that last dress you got today, your cherry is not only getting popped, it is getting obliterated," Alex teased.

"Should I wear it?" Charlie looked unsure.

"Definitely!" Val and Alex agreed.

"Okay. You guys. I'm a bit freaked out right now. I don't know what to expect. I mean, well, I know what to expect, but I don't. Does that make any sense whatsoever?"

"Don't worry! You've come to the best place to get advice and words of encouragement."

"And caution." Alex stared across the bar to where Ryder sat on a barstool chatting with Logan and Sera.

"No. No caution is needed. Don't go there, Alex. Not tonight. Tonight is about Charlie."

"You're right. I'm sorry."

"It's alright. Alex, I do hope one of these days you will feel comfortable enough with me to share what all the animosity is between you and Ryder. I promise I'm a good listener."

Alex smiled at her new friend. "One day, I will. I promise. But Val is right. Tonight is about you. Back to Friday night. Neither of us have ever dated Jax so we can't pull from personal experience as to what he's attracted to, but I think it is safe to say he is majorly attracted to you."

"Yes," Charlie laughed, I think that is a very safe assumption. I didn't really understand why until tonight. I mean, I know he thinks I'm beautiful. I'm naive, but even I know I'm a good-looking person. But I figured out what else it is he is drawn to. Jaxon is a sapiosexual."

"Hold up. Jaxon is a what?"

"He's a sapiosexual. A sapiosexual is someone who is attracted to or aroused by the intelligence of someone. I think he's attracted to my brain."

"That sounds about right. If there were ever anyone who would be attracted to a brain, it would be Jax. He is a geek through and through. You've seen that monstrosity of a command center he works at all day, right?" Alex shook her head.

"Yes. It is quite substantial."

"Well, let's hope after Friday night you can say the same about his cock!"

"There's just no stopping you tonight, is there?" Once again Val shook her head in disbelief.

"Nope! I'm on a roll. You know what? Sera is right. This calls for shots! And, before we get too trashed, I want to hear more about this sapiosexual thing."

Jax peeled himself out of his jeans and climbed into the steamy shower. As the water began to stream down his body and the lather of his soap began to cleanse, he couldn't help but think of Charlie and their encounter. He was having a hard time believing he had so little control over his reaction to her. In his mind, this was just one more indication that she was meant to be his, that they were meant to be together.

As he stepped out of the shower, he heard his phone alarm go off. His heart began to race as he realized it was the sound he had assigned to the alerts he set up about Charlie. Wrapping a towel around his waist, his hair still dripping and skin still wet, he hurried to his office and slid behind his computer screens. In a matter of seconds, he had the alert pulled up. The private investigators her family had hired were good and they were beginning to narrow down her location.

"Well, we can't have that now, can we?"

Slowly and methodically, Jaxon began laying more false trails in the hope they would lead the investigators away from Ouray. For the better part of two hours he plotted, planned, and played with the information he threw out like breadcrumbs. By the time he was done, he had made it appear Charlie had never actually left the East Coast. Instead, it now appeared she had zig-zagged her way down the coast into Florida and then taken a flight to the Cayman Islands.

As he added more alerts to his alarm system, he knew, at least for now, he had bought her more time. If the investigators were truly as good as they appeared to be, he wouldn't be able to way-lay them much longer. All he could do now was keep watching, waiting, and veering them off course as often as possible.

With that task temporarily taken care of, he called for Chewy and began their nightly routine. He had just crawled into bed when a text came through.

Charlie
> Are you awake?

Jax
> Hello, Little Rabbit.

Charlie
> I just wanted to tell you I'm looking forward to Friday night.

Jax
> So am I. You should get some rest.

Charlie
> Is that a hint of things to come?

Jax
> Quite possibly. Charlie…how drunk are you?

Charlie
> I can still form coherent thoughts, but definitely over my limit.

> **Jax:** Take your aspirin. Drink your water. Get some sleep.

> **Charlie:** That sounds very dominant energy of you. Are you a dom?

> **Jax:** Oh, you definitely have had too much to drink. We can talk doms and subs and other kinky subjects another time. You have so much to learn and experience, Little Rabbit. But we're going to take it slow. Right now, you're going to be a good little rabbit and go to bed.

> **Charlie:** Alright. Goodnight, Jax.

> **Jax:** Goodnight.

As Jax laid his phone down, he grinned. Doms and subs. Silly little rabbit. Her naivety delighted him and made him unbelievably excited. Lying there, scenes of what might one day happen between them scrolled through his mind. He wanted to share so much with her. But first, he thought, she deserves her initial sexual encounter to be a truly memorable experience – a romantic experience. She deserves candlelight, soft music, and tenderness. He intended to be gentle with her.

Scaring her off by going too far and too fast was the absolute last thing he wanted to do.

No. He wanted Charlie to want to stay.

In his heart and mind, he knew they belonged together and he was determined to make that happen. Nobody was going to scare her off and nobody was going to take her away. If they even tried, there would be hell to pay.

Chapter Thirteen

Charlie stood staring at the wisp of a dress she'd been talked into buying. Butterflies fluttered in her stomach as she thought of draping the silky material over her body and being bold enough to answer the door for Jaxon. She'd almost felt like an imposter the couple of other times she'd gone out with her friends and worn Sera's dresses.

This time, the dress belonged to her. Though she'd had her initial doubts about purchasing it, she was now filled with excited anticipation at the thought of wearing it and then having it peeled from her body with slow seduction.

At least, she hoped that was on the agenda for the night.

She was ready. She was more than ready. While she and Jax barely knew each other, she knew without a doubt she wanted him to be her first and maybe even her only. She was seriously attracted to him. Who wouldn't be? But she kept finding herself questioning her feelings for him. All she'd ever done was read about love. What if this was just lust disguised in an abundance of like? What if most of what she felt for him was wrapped up in gratitude for sheltering her during her time of need and helping her to begin her new life? Everything was happening so quickly. What if her feelings, whatever they truly turned out to be, were just temporary?

Worst of all, what if her friends were wrong, what if she were wrong, and he didn't reciprocate the love she thought was in her heart?

It was overwhelming to think about.

Taking a deep breath, she slipped the dress off the hanger and onto her body, arranging and re-arranging each piece until it lay as she wanted. She left her freshly washed and dried hair hanging loose, the long, golden strands a perfectly straight curtain that stopped at her waist. She left her face clean with the exception of smudging up her eyes a bit to make them pop and a touch of lipgloss. Heels and minimal jewelry were next and as she slipped her feet into the shoes and began to wrap the strappy leather around her ankles, her confidence began to grow.

She glanced at the time as she picked up her favorite scent and dabbed it at her wrists, her neck, and down the exposed valley between her breasts. Then, taking a deep breath and squaring her shoulders, she glanced in the mirror and looked herself over from head to toe.

Yes, she thought. There would be no doubt with the way she looked that she was on board for a night of seduction. When the knock on her door came a moment later, a confident grin spread across her face.

Antsy. He would have never described himself as such, but there was absolutely no other word that fit better as he stood on the landing outside Charlie's apartment and waited for her to answer the door. He hadn't been able to think of anything but her all day. Every time he had tried to get work done or take care of one thing or another around the house, he'd found himself daydreaming about their impending night.

He'd done the responsible thing and taken Chewy to Ryder's. He intended to be way too busy to provide proper care and attention to his dog for the night. While he would have opted for Logan and Sera to dog sit, Ryder had been the better choice as he was going to need Sera's help later.

He was just about to knock again when the door to the apartment opened and revealed Charlie standing there bundled in her coat and ready to go. The mild disappointment he felt at not seeing what she'd chosen to wear for the evening vanished quickly.

"Hello, Little Rabbit." Jax leaned in the doorway and gently placed his lips on her cheek. "It appears you're ready to go. Shall we?" He held his large hand out to her and she looked up at him with a beaming grin as she placed her hand in his.

"Yes. Yes, I'm ready."

Jax held the door for Charlie as she stepped into The Gold Rush. The sweet scent of her perfume tickled his nose and he took another deep breath, savoring the aroma. He wanted to have every moment of the night branded into his mind. Though he truly wanted to take her to someplace new, the idea of being too far from her apartment held no appeal. It only made sense to keep close to Ouray for the evening so he could carry out his plans.

Knowing what he had in store for them for the remainder of the night made even the necessary wait while they had dinner almost unendurable. Adding driving time from another location was unacceptable.

They stepped to the hostess stand and Jax gave his name while simultaneously reaching for Charlie to help her from her heavy coat. He thought nothing of it when she peeked up at him under demure lashes and opened the sash on the coat. But as the material slipped from her shoulders, he felt his mouth dry up and the blood rush from his brain straight to his cock. The perfectly placed scraps of silk left little to the imagination and it was all he could do to keep from falling to his knees in awe.

The shimmering peach, almost sheer material, lay behind her neck before draping loosely across her breasts and disappearing behind her back. It then wrapped around her body and fell enticingly across the indention of her waist where it miraculously turned into the tiniest skirt he'd ever seen. The dress, if you could call it that, made it perfectly clear that the woman before him was built like a goddess. Her high and tight, perfectly rounded breasts needed no support and the outline of her puckered nipples made his mouth water. Her hourglass figure was everything he'd been dreaming of for weeks.

No. There would be no more waiting. She was going to be his tonight.

If he had his way? She would be his – always.

When he heard the hostess gasp and let out a low whistle, Jax snapped out of the paralysis of his erotic stupor.

"Charlie," he pleaded, "are you trying to kill me?"

She tilted her head and smiled up at him teasingly. "Whatever do you mean, Jaxon?" When she batted her lashes at him, she sent a thrill of anticipation running down his spine. He couldn't help but grin back at her knowingly.

Yes, he thought, tonight is the night.

Sitting through dinner had been an exercise in patience. The sexual tension that surged between them all evening reached a fever pitch of yearning long before they finished their meal. The longer the meal had lasted, the more the ache between her legs had spread.

Charlie wasn't sure what all was going on throughout her body. Anxious anticipation mixed with an overdose of arousal made a strange combination of sexual need bubbling under a haze of uncertainty. She wanted Jax. She wanted this. She wanted what was to come.

And while part of her wanted to think further, to think into the future, she forced herself to concentrate on the present.

Now, with key in hand, she reached for the doorknob of her apartment. When Jax closed the distance between them, pressing her back to his large body and reached around her to open the door, she all but melted back against him. Her legs shook, not from the cold, but from apprehension, from urgency, from desire she could no longer control.

His lips brushed against her neck as he opened the door wide and then, in tandem, they stepped through the doorway and out of the cold.

"Mmm...Little Rabbit. You smell sinfully amazing." Jax's arms circled her waist and untied her sash. As he slid the coat from her shoulders, she started to step away and into the living room, but he caught her and hauled her back against him as he placed her coat on the hook by the door, and did the same with his own. "Not so fast. We've got all night, Charlie."

She turned in his arms and looked up into his eyes, flames of desire burning in the depths of the intense blue.

"Jax, I don't know what to do. I mean, I do, but I don't." The smile that lit his face instantly relaxed her.

"You don't have to be nervous. You don't have to worry. I've got you and I promise to take excellent care of you."

"I know you will, but I…"

"Shhh…" Jax pressed her against the wall of the vestibule, caging her body in, and then claimed her mouth. His lips, soft and demanding, instantly made her crave more. She grabbed onto his waist, holding tightly to keep from sliding to the floor as her body turned liquid under his commanding presence, his seeking tongue. She couldn't help but feel she was in for an experience she would never forget – and all they'd done so far was kiss. What, she wondered, would it feel like to have his lips on more of her body? What would it feel like when he was inside of her?

She knew to expect a bit of pain, at least initially. She also knew Jax would do everything in his power to make it less painful, to make it as amazing as possible. But her inquisitive mind wouldn't be satisfied until she'd taken those steps.

She was ready for more. She was in need of more. The urgency she felt began to seep through as she kissed him back – each of them diving deeply, searching and exploring.

Her mind kept going back to the moment at the restaurant and the raw hunger that had been on Jaxon's face when he'd removed her coat. Now, the hunger was stronger than ever.

Her hands began to roam and just as she'd done in the storage room of the bar, she reached for his ass. Jerking back, he grabbed her hands to stop her. His breathing ragged as he looked into her eyes, he locked her arms over her head and dove back into her mouth. The realization of why he'd stopped her made her giddy.

She'd never known what having power over a man felt like. If, she wondered, such a small move could push him so far, so quickly, what more could she possibly do to make him feel good? To push him further? To give him pleasure?

She was ready to learn.

His lips moved from her mouth down her throat, kissing, licking. The moans of approval from deep within his chest echoed around them, and as they did, her arousal began to slowly trickle from her pussy – an uncontrollable lava flow of desire.

He pulled back, releasing her hands, and stood there a moment, staring at her. She looked him up and down, just as he did her, and when her eyes landed on the bulge in his pants, they widened in newly realized wonder. How exactly was that going to fit inside of her?

Yes, she'd seen him naked but he hadn't been hard then. Now, the absolutely massive tent protruding from his body made her question the logistics of having sex with him.

"You're thinking too hard, Charlie. Do I need to kiss all the thoughts from your head? Make your brain go fuzzy so you do nothing more than feel?"

She couldn't think, she couldn't speak. All she could do was continue to stare. When at last she looked up at him, it was with awe.

"Alright. That's it." Jax scooped her into his arms and carried her into the living room. It was only then that she realized there were lit candles scattered throughout the room, the small kitchen, and, she noted as he continued further into the apartment, in the bedroom, as well.

"What? How?"

"My sister is a hopeless romantic. I sent her a text as we were leaving the restaurant. She was here on standby ready to help set the scene."

"Wow! My first seduction ever made even more romantic by the queen of seduction herself!"

"I won't read her books, but that doesn't mean I won't take advantage of her knowledge." Jax sat on the bed and cradled her in his lap. "Knowledge like this. He reached for a remote on her nightstand and with the press of a button, romantic music filled the room.

"This is perfect, Jax."

"No. Not yet it isn't. But I promise you it will be." Their lips met again and the hunger not yet sated roared to life once more. Jax laid her on the bed and broke the kiss. With their chests heaving he asked, "Birth control? I brought condoms. I'm totally clean, but I don't think pregnancy is an option either of us want to entertain at this point."

"I've been on birth control since I was fourteen. My irregular periods freaked my mother out and she was determined I wouldn't defile our good name with an out-of-wedlock baby. You don't need the condom unless you don't trust me."

"I trust you, Little Rabbit. And while I don't necessarily agree with your mother's thought process, I'm glad she protected you."

"Agreed."

"Now. Tell me something..." Jax looked ravenously down her body and then back up again. "Do you think you achieved your goal with your dress tonight?"

Charlie's cheeks heated, a crimson blush that slowly spread down her neck and prickled along her chest.

"Don't answer that. Let me share with you exactly what seeing you in this peachy concoction did to me." He grabbed her hand and brought the back of it to his lips. Then looking into her eyes, he pulled her hand down to rest on the hard length of his cock.

Her eyes widened in shock. Even through his pants, she could tell what she thought was an impressive bulge was just the tip of the iceberg. His sharp intake of breath told her he was as anxious as she was to take things to the next level.

Leaving her hand on his cock, he reached for the edge of the material covering one of her breasts and began gliding his fingers along the outline. "Do you have any idea just how difficult it was for me to sit across from you tonight and look at you, at your breasts, these perfectly rounded globes just barely being covered by the tiniest excuse for a dress I've ever seen? Your nipples were hard all night. Believe me, I was looking."

As he spoke, he began to trace first one nipple, then the other. Back and forth he went, pleasuring her with nothing more than the tip of his finger. Her nipples had never been so hard, the stiff peaks aching for more, though she didn't know just yet what the more might be.

"I don't know exactly how I'm supposed to take this off of you, to unwrap you, but I'm going to go with what I've imagined doing all evening" He leaned forward then and licked the valley between her breasts, tracing her sternum with his soft tongue and leaving a warm, damp trail behind. Then biting the edge of the material covering one breast, he tugged gently and slowly revealed her heavy breast and perfectly taut nipple. He repeated the process on the other side until her upper body was bared to him.

"Jax..." Charlie attempted to cover up but her hand was quickly caught in his.

"Please don't. Let me look at you, Charlie."

With a deep breath, she lowered her arm. And though she began to relax once more, he didn't let go of her hand – an anchor as she experienced each new sensation.

Then, with his eyes on hers, never wavering, he lowered his head to her breast and licked the stiffened peak of her nipple. Charlie moaned with pleasure. More. She wanted more of that, and she only had to wait a couple of seconds for Jax to comply.

Again he licked, and his tongue began to flick. More, she thought. More. She simply couldn't get enough. Then he gently sucked her nipple in his mouth and when he did she felt more of her arousal begin to dampen the tops of her thighs.

But it was the next moment that almost made her dizzy with pleasure.

Jax sucked hard and her body bowed off the bed, she gasped out his name and when she did, he growled deeply and shifted. He maneuvered until he was sitting on his knees between her legs. He caressed her calves, her outer thighs, and back down.

Lost. She was lost in sensation and she knew there was more to come. With her eyes open and staring at the ceiling, heart racing, she waited, ready and wanting – anticipating his next move but unsure of what it would be.

"Look at me, Charlie." She glanced down and when she did she felt as if time stood still. "Raise up on your elbows and truly look at me." She did as he asked and when she looked at his face she became lost in his eyes – caught in his gaze, she couldn't look away.

"I'm going to taste you, Little Rabbit. I'm going to see just how sweet you truly are. You are going to watch me, watch my head between your legs, watch my mouth pleasuring you. I'm not going to stop until you cum. And when you do, I'm going to keep eating your sweet pussy until you scream for me to stop. Even then I'm going to continue until I've had my fill. You see, this is about bringing you pleasure, but also about getting my own. Because, Charlie, if you're as sweet as I think you're going to be, I'm never going to get my fill."

"Oh, God..."

With his hands on her knees, he gently spread her legs. The slip of a skirt attached to her dress had already shifted, sneaking further and further up her body, and now, with her legs spread wide, the material gave up any hope of staying in place and rolled to her waist.

She watched his reaction and preened when his eyes met hers with molten desire flashing in their depths.

This man, she thought, is going to be the death of me.

Chapter Fourteen

Jax thought he'd died and gone to heaven. Spreading her legs slowly had been a lesson in patience and the reward was mind-blowing.

Bare.

Not only did she not have on any kind of underwear, but she was bare. Her pussy showed no trace of hair and he was certain when he finally touched her there he would find her skin even more smooth than the rest of her body.

His cock throbbed, begging for attention.

After losing it in the storeroom the other day, he was trying his hardest to keep things under control. Tonight was about giving her everything, and he was determined he wasn't going to embarrass himself by coming prematurely.

He had a full night planned for them and for now, his cock was going to have to take a backseat and wait its turn.

"Holy fuck..." Jax couldn't take his eyes off her. Scooting down until his face was mere inches from her pussy, he inhaled and let the sweet aroma permeate his senses. She was wet. She was more than wet – she was dripping. He was ready to lap every last drop from her, to drain her until his thirst was slaked.

He glanced up to see if she was still watching as he'd asked and when her half-lidded gaze met his, he grinned mischievously. Without breaking eye contact, he stuck out his tongue and licked between her folds, bottom to top, slowly, teasingly. She gasped and released a tiny squeal of delight.

It spurred him on.

Again, he licked, gathering her hot liquid on his tongue and savoring each drop. When another gush of honey came from her body, he latched on, diving deeply with his tongue straight into her center.

His tongue pleasured her as he devoured. He couldn't ever remember being so starved for someone. He took his time, enjoying himself immensely, but knowing she needed release, he came up for air and went to work on her clit. The protruding nub begged for attention and he was more than willing to answer the call. His tongue licked one side and then the other, and with each lick her body jerked in response. Side to side, top to bottom, and when he began to work his tongue in a circle, her legs began to tremble.

He felt it coming, felt it building. And when her orgasm hit, it was like a bomb detonating. She gasped, she moaned, she called out his name, and when she did, he felt as if he'd died and gone to heaven. He swore there was no sweeter sound than his name on her lips as she came.

"Jax!"

More. He wanted more. She needed more. He never stopped – his tongue brought her untold pleasures, and knowing he was giving her her first true sexual experience made him lightheaded.

Her sensitivity sky-rocketed and her legs clamped down on his head – and still he didn't stop. Looping his arms around her legs and locking them in place, he opened her wider and put her even more on display. A buffet of delights, her pussy was at his mercy.

She begged him to stop but her pleas didn't last. Within moments those pleas changed direction and she began to beg him for more.

His cock was solid steel. He ached to be inside her. But though he throbbed with need, he wanted her to come again. He wanted to feel her pussy throbbing on his face once more, her body bucking as he swallowed all she would give him.

It didn't take long. Instinctively, he knew what she needed to chase that high one more time. He suckled, he teased, he licked, and then he repeated. When he felt her climbing again, he let loose a low growl. The vibration in combination with his loving shot her up and over the peak in a heartbeat. Her body bowed off the bed once more and she gripped the comforter tightly with both hands as she flew.

Quickly, Jax released her and undressed. He was back between her legs and kissing up her body before she ever even knew he'd gone. As he kissed, leaving a trail of wetness from her orgasm, he spoke to her.

Preparation was still key. He knew he still needed to go slow. Her orgasms were wanted, necessary, and though they undoutably made her tighter, they would ultimately serve to relax her body enough to fully take him in.

"Charlie. My little rabbit. Are you ready?" Her voice was a whisper, her breathing not yet under control.

"More, Jax. I need more."

He couldn't hide his smile – not the one on his lips, the one beaming from his eyes, or the one spreading in his heart. Charlie was his – whether she knew it or not.

With his face above hers and his body nestled between her legs, he felt as if he was home.

"I need you to open those beautiful eyes and look at me, Charlie." She blinked once, twice, and then finally focused on his face. "I'm doing all I can to prepare you, but this is still going to cause you some discomfort – at least initially. I swear to you I'll go slow. We'll go slow. I don't want to hurt you. Not ever, Little Rabbit."

"It's okay, Jaxon. I'm ready. I'm ready for you."

Her words said she was ready but he could feel the tension thrumming throughout her body. Braced on his arms so he wouldn't crush her, he kissed her softly. Tenderly his lips pressed against her, his tongue tracing along the seam of her lips until she opened for him. When she did, his tongue began exploring – tasting, savoring, tangling with hers. He let his hunger for her pour into the kiss until he felt her muscles begin to relax, her body slowly begin to go lax beneath him.

He changed the angle of the kiss and as he did, he began to press the hard length of his cock into her heat. He rubbed up and down, coating himself in the slickness that remained from her orgasms. Then slowly, ever so slowly, he pushed the bulbous head against her, feeling her opening as it began to give, to widen slightly for him. He pulled back and reached between them, grabbed his cock, and rubbed it up and down in her juices once more, making sure he was well lubricated. Then he pushed in again, further this time, stretching her more and more.

And as he probed her pussy, testing her limits, he watched her face. The barrier was there. He could feel it. But when nothing but pure bliss was written in her features, he gave into his own need and pushed past the constraints of her virginity. She gasped in surprise and her breath caught as she processed the combination of pain and pleasure, and he held still so as to give her a moment. He paused for her to catch her breath and watched and waited as her body accepted his intrusion.

"Are you alright, Charlie? Did I hurt you?"

"No. No, Jax. You didn't hurt me. Just...just give me a moment."

"All the time you need, Little Rabbit. Tell me when you're ready. I'll wait for you. Always."

He didn't have to wait long. A few deep breaths and a moment later she nodded her head at him to continue. Once again, he kissed her, giving her a bit more time to get acclimated to his girth. And when she responded and began wiggling her hips against him, he knew it was time.

With another big push, he seated himself inside her fully, pausing to let her feel him again. Then he pulled most of the way out of her and entered her once more.

The execution was smoother, less painful, and he began to relax. The worst of her pain was past. Now, he thought, it was time to give her, give them both, the pleasure they'd been waiting for.

A few more slow, intentional strokes, and then he set up a rhythm, slowly fucking her, letting her begin to feel what it was truly like to make love. Each time he entered her he felt as if he went a bit further, that her body accepted his a bit more.

It was a magical moment in his eyes and he hoped with every fiber of his being it was a magical moment in hers.

His body demanded he go harder, to fuck her harder, but his heart wouldn't let him. He continued to stroke her methodically, hoping she would become accustomed to the feel of their bodies joining, but soon it was more than he could handle. When he finally gave in to his need to pump inside her hard and fast, she was right there with him, her hips rising to meet his. They raced each other to the finish line.

He rested his forehead against hers as they moved together. "Look at me, Charlie. Look in my eyes." When she did, he told her, "We go together. This time, we both fly."

Her nod was barely perceptible, but when she gave it, he gave in to the uncontrollable urge to pound her and fill her with his cum. With his control all shot to hell, he went for it, and within only a moment, he felt his balls tighten, his orgasm beginning to zing up through his shaft, and his cock hardening further than he ever thought possible. When the walls of her pussy clamped down on him, he lost it. He slammed home one final time and together they fell into a sea of orgasmic bliss.

Charlie swore every nerve ending in her body was on fire. Her mind kept repeating the phrase 'holy fuck,' like a mantra. Her heart pounded so hard in her chest that the throbbing beat echoed in her ears and her chest heaved as her lungs tried to catch up to her breathing. Is that how it always was? Her mind raced as she marveled. If it was, how on earth would she ever survive?

It was amazing. It was intense. It was...everything.

She wanted more.

As she lay there with her eyes closed absorbing the sensations that pulsed throughout her body, she wondered what came next. When she felt Jaxon's lips press to hers, his tongue probing against her lips, she opened for him and sighed internally at the much-welcomed intrusion.

Tenderly they kissed, sealing the magic of the moment in their memories. Then she felt him pull back and she opened her eyes to find him staring at her. He moved, shifting slightly, and then pulled out of her. His eyes never left hers, watching, waiting, evaluating, as if he was trying to determine how she was after their encounter.

It made her heart smile to know he was so concerned.

He rolled off her then and wrapping his arms around her, pulled her against him and curled his large body around hers. It was like she was all wrapped up in a Jaxon burrito. Contentment washed over her and she smiled as she wiggled back against him.

Jax spoke softly, his lips close to her ear and his warm breath sending tingles down her spine, "Careful there, Little Rabbit. You'll get things going again and we should probably give us both a bit of recovery time."

"So, does that..."

"Shhh...My brain needs recovery time, too, Charlie."

She couldn't help the small giggle that escaped nor the huge grin that spread across her face. Her inquisitive mind had so many questions, but for the moment, she was perfectly content to lay in his arms and savor the experience. She closed her eyes and a replay of the evening began to run through her mind. A moment later she heard soft snoring and even breathing.

The idea of sleeping in his arms appealed to her in so many ways and as it did, she let her body begin to drift and soon joined him in peaceful slumber.

The hazy in-between of sleep and wakefulness clouded Charlie's mind. Her brain demanded more rest but for some reason, her body was suddenly awake. It didn't take long for her to realize the cause of her abrupt arrival back into the land of awareness.

Jax's lips kissed her neck, his tongue licking lazy strokes up, down, and back again, and when he reached her ear, he sucked the lobe into his mouth and flicked his tongue against it. His arms still encircled her body, but his hands were no longer still. Arms crossed on her stomach, he cupped each breast in his hands and his thumbs gently teased her nipples. As the stiff peaks formed, he moaned and the deep rumble shot down her spine in an arrow of desire straight to her pussy.

Jax began to grind against her and she could feel the hard length of his cock as it probed against the small of her back. It thrilled her when she realized the wetness she felt was his pre-cum.

He had obviously recovered and was ready for more. Though she despised abrupt wakeups, this was an allowable and very welcomed exception.

He whispered her name against her ear and she licked and bit her lip at the sexiness of her name flowing from his incredibly deep voice.

"Charlie..."

"Jax..."

"Let me in."

She nodded and when she did, his hand left her breast and trailed softly down her side, her hip. Then his large palm smoothed down her ass cheek to her thigh and pulled her leg up. A mere second later and she felt the blunt head of his cock as he coated himself once more in the combined remnants of their earlier loving and the hot gush of her arousal.

He positioned himself at her entrance and then asked, "Are you ready, Little Rabbit?"

She moaned as she answered, "Yes!"

Jax immediately buried himself inside her, slamming his dick hard and fast into her heat. They each gasped as the sensations overwhelmed them. Then he pulled out and did it again. With hard, purposeful strokes he filled her time and again.

She could do nothing more than hold on as he took her to new heights. Having him enter her from behind was different – the angle, the feeling, the depth. She swore in that moment she felt more alive and in tune with the world around her than she had ever been in her entire life.

Then he reached between them, and as he continued to fuck her, he began to play with her clit. His fingers stroked, they teased, they lightly pinched, and before Charlie knew it, she was lost in orgasm again. Stars exploded behind her eyes and she felt her pussy clamp down hard on his cock.

"God, yes!" Jax groaned in her ear as he slammed home again and again. "More. I need more. I want to give you more."

His fingers never stopped and neither did his cock. Soon she felt herself opening even further and when she did, she felt him hit a new spot deep inside her. She gasped and her eyes rolled back in her head.

"What...What's that... Oh, God!"

"Oh, yeah... There it is. Hold on tight, Little Rabbit."

She wasn't sure what he did, but with a few more strokes, she came hard, her body shooting out of orbit. She couldn't hold back the cries of pleasure and beneath her euphoria she heard him as he lost control and flew with her.

"Fuck! Fuck! Fuck! Holy fuck!!!"

She felt his cock begin to orgasm deep inside her, each surge filling her with his hot cum. With each pulse of his cock, she felt her pussy walls clench down on him over and over, milking him for all he could give her.

When he stilled, buried to the hilt inside her, her breath caught in her throat and her eyes rolled back in her head. She swore she was on the verge of passing out when she heard Jax talking to her.

"Breathe, baby. You've got to breathe." As she gasped for air, she felt him begin to rub her body, his hands trying to relax her and bring her down from her high. "Breathe with me, Charlie. In. Out. In. Out. There you go. That's it." Her body was still bowed tightly but her breathing slowly began to return to normal. "Now. As much as I love your pussy clamped down on my cock, you're going to have to relax, baby. That's it. Relax, Little Rabbit, so I can pull out of you."

Bit by bit she felt her body begin to go lax, her muscles releasing the stranglehold they held on his cock in small increments. Each time she thought her body done, a small spasm would hit and clamp down on him once again. Eventually, she began to float and when she did, Jax pulled out of her and cuddled closely once more.

"What was that, Jax?"

A soft chuckle came from deep within his chest. "That, Charlotte Grace Abbingdon, was an out-of-body experience."

"Can we do it again?"

"Oh, I plan on us doing that as often as we can."

She yawned and snuggled closer once again. As she drifted off, Jax's deep, contented laugh floated around her and lulled her to sleep.

Chapter Fifteen

Charlie stood naked in front of the bathroom sink and looked at her reflection in the mirror, studying her features carefully. Did she look different? Would people be able to look at her and know she was no longer a virgin?

She certainly felt different even though she still felt like herself. She just felt more...alive. She felt more complete. She felt sensual and sexy and more in charge of her body, her life, than she'd ever felt before.

The aroma of freshly brewed coffee reached her nose just as her phone signaled an incoming text message. She reached for a towel to dry off her freshly showered body and wrapped it around herself before she went to retrieve her phone. She grinned as she read the message.

Sera

> Margs 2night. Your place. I've got the margs. Alex has the chips. Val the queso and salsa. You have the story. Need details but not too many because... brother. See you at 6!

Charlie

> 6 works. See you all then.

Alex

> ALL the details. Bringing brownies too, because chocolate is necessary after a night of getting your brains fucked out.

Val

> Alex!

Sera

> Alex!

Alex

> I always get picked on. You know you guys were thinking it. I'm just the only one who had the balls to say it.

Sera

> Your balls ought to be clamped sometimes! Yeesh! What if she doesn't want to give us ALL the details?

> **Alex**
> That's what the tequila is for.

> **Val**
> SMDH…We'll see you tonight, Charlie.

She was standing there giggling over their messages when Jax walked in with a steaming mug of coffee in each hand.

"And just what has you so tickled this early in the morning?" He handed her one of the mugs and she took a small sip before she answered.

"It appears I'm hosting girls' night tonight."

"Ah, I see. You're having your first Dickscussion."

"My what? I don't know what that is." Confused, Charlie waited for an explanation.

"A Dickscussion. It's where all you girls get together and discuss the first time you have sex with someone, or some special night that was planned that ended in sex. You get to do both of those and because it was your first time ever having sex, that's a triple word score, Little Rabbit."

"I see. I have so much to learn."

Jax leaned in and kissed her. "Mmm. I'll do all I can to thoroughly instruct you."

"Yeah, well, I'm a fast learner." The impish grin she gave him worked as she hoped it would.

"Oh, I know." Jax set both their coffee cups on her dresser and walked toward her with a glint in his eye. She squealed in delight as he picked her up and tossed her over his shoulder before carrying her to the bed. He plopped her down and with a mischievous look in his eyes, climbed on top of her, a wolf stalking his prey. "Let's see how well you retain what you learn..."

Her giggles soon turned to moans of pleasure, and true to his word, Charlie received another detailed instruction she would never forget.

The whirlwind that came swirling through Charlie's door later that evening left her head spinning in wonder. The three women, who had opened their arms, their hearts, and accepted her into their circle without thinking twice, came carrying everything you could possibly need for an amazing night of fun girl talk.

As they unpacked their food and drink, loaded trays, and began mixing their refreshments, it was as if a well-rehearsed play were unfolding before her eyes. Though they talked and laughed and sometimes spoke over each other, no words were necessary as they coordinated the presentation of their spread.

Girl dinner to the max!

Alex scooped a large dollop of queso on her tortilla chip and toasted with it before she took a bite. "Alright, bitches! We have food. We have drinks. We need details! We need all the sexy, down-and-dirty details! Fill us in, Charlie!"

"No!," Sera yelped. "I do NOT need all that. Dear God! Please, don't go into that much detail!"

Val spoke up, "Just tell us if it was everything you imagined it would be. Was it?"

The dreamy look that washed over Charlie's face spoke volumes. "I don't think I've ever dreamed anything so absolutely perfect."

"Oooh! Y'all see that? That right there, ladies, is the look of bliss. And while I'm trying my hardest not to think about the fact that it was my brother that put that look on your face, I'm also fucking proud of my brother for putting that look on your face."

"I still want details," Alex pouted as she shoved another chip in her mouth.

"I," Charlie paused, "I can't even begin to describe how wonderful it all was, how special he made me feel. And when he..." she glanced at Sera, "well, let's just say I saw stars. No! It was more than stars. It was like phosphenes – you know, all the luminous stars, colors, and swirls you see when you rub your eyes a little too hard. Yeah. It was definitely like that."

"Now we're talkin'!"

"I mean, I have nothing other than my solo experiences to compare it to, but I can tell you that it was infinitely more mind-blowing than anything I've managed on my own."

"So, is Jax hung?"

"Alex!" All three women exclaimed at once.

"Y'all can stop giving me a hard time. If it were anyone other than Jax, y'all would have wanted a play-by-play and measurements!"

"Is that what normally would happen at a Dickscussion?" Charlie asked.

"Dickscussion? Where did you get that from?" Val laughed.

"Jax said that's what this girls' night is tonight. A Dickscussion."

"Ah, I see." Sera contemplated for a moment. " I don't know that I've ever thought of putting a name on it before now, but I think I prefer 'Post-Coital Parlay.'

"Cock Confab?" Alex interjected.

Sera snorted as she giggled, "Dicked-down Deliberation?"

"No, no, no," Val laughed. "Railing Repartee!"

Hilarity filled the apartment and as the night wore on, the euphemisms and possible names became more and more outlandish. Long after her friends had gone home, echoes of their good times continued to ring in her ears and her sides ached from laughter.

Jax lay stretched out on Ryder's sofa, a half-drank bottle of beer in his hand. Logan sat sideways with his knees hooked over the arm of Ryder's lone living room chair munching on corn chips, while Ryder lay on the floor beside Chewy who was eyeing the bottle he drank from, hopeful he would get a taste.

"Your dog wants some beer."

"Do NOT give my dog any beer."

"He just wants to be one of the guys." Ryder ruffled the thick fur, "Don't ya, Chewy?"

"He is one of the guys – at least for another month or so."

"Ouch." Logan grimaced as he looked down at the mountain of fluff.

"Yeah, well, it has to happen. He and I have had a long discussion about it and as much as it pains me to do it, in more ways than one, he has to get fixed. One giant furball is enough. I don't need to be bankrolling his child support all over the damn mountain."

"Should we be worried about you having to pay child support? You know I offer a friends and family discount for representation, right?"

"Shut up, Ry. And no, she's covered." The corner of Jax's mouth quirked up, evidence of just how happy he was with the outcome of the night before.

"Awe, hell. Look at his sappy puss, Logan. Just look at him. I swear to God it's contagious. You go and fall for Sera; now this asshole has fallen, and hard from the looks of it. You guys need to get the hell out of my house before you infect me."

"No. You need to stop being an asshole and be happy for us." Logan threw a chip at him which never reached its target as the dog intercepted it.

"No. What he needs to do is have that fucking discussion with Alex."

"You can stop right there. Alex is in the past and that's where I'm keeping her."

"Dude. Just tell her what happened. It's long past time that you came clean with her and you guys came to an understanding."

"Jax, you know I can't. I can't break her heart that way. If she ever finds out she will be devastated."

"He's right, man. She deserves to know."

"And just how would either of you feel knowing the only parent you had growing up betrayed you and threw your boyfriend in jail for no God damn good reason? And on fucking prom night? The night you'd been dreaming about forever? I can't tell her that her dad did that to me, to us. Isn't it bad enough that she had to grow up without her mother? I won't say I'm glad the old man is dead and gone because that's just a horrible way to think and feel. What I will say is that I'm glad she has the girls, and now, your girl to lean on."

"Ry. She knows her dad was an ass at times. She just doesn't know he was an ass to you."

"How the hell did tonight become about me? This is Jax's night to be given shit. Let's shift gears here."

"True enough. So, Jax...since it's obvious that you've fallen for Charlie, don't you think you need to fill us in on her backstory? You said there might be trouble. Will there be?"

"I'm trying my hardest to keep that from happening. I'll fill you in, but I need you two to swear what I tell you will not leave this room."

"You know whatever you tell us goes no further, right Ryder?"

"You don't even have to question that, my man. Blood brothers, through and through."

"Alright. So, here's the thing..."

Jax didn't feel the least bit guilty leaving Chewy with Ryder for another night. It was late, and though he and Charlie had been together earlier in the day, he felt he'd been away from her way too long. The few hours they'd been apart felt like years. The need he had for her, to be with her, was overwhelming. But instead of running scared, as he was sure he would have done in the past, he was running toward the woman he wanted and hoped to build a future with.

He couldn't put his finger on just exactly what it was that drew him to her or how it had happened so quickly, but he knew without a doubt she was the one. As best as he could tell, she was, quite simply, made for him. Beautiful, intelligent, sexy, kind, caring – the list could go on forever. It was as if someone had taken everything he'd ever looked for in a woman, dumped it all into a gorgeously wrapped package, and tied a big red bow on top.

She was a gift fate had led to his door and deposited in his arms. As long as she would have him, he intended to keep her, care for her, and love her for the rest of their lives.

Sharing his concerns with his best friends earlier in the evening helped to relieve his mind about her situation. He knew Logan and Ryder would keep her secrets and would also be on the lookout for anything unusual that might pop up in Ouray. They'd always had each other's backs. That was something he'd always been able to count on.

Now, with explicit thoughts of what he intended to do once he had Charlie back in his arms, Jax ran up the stairs to her apartment, taking the steps two at a time.

―――*ℓℓ*―――

Charlie crawled into bed and pulled the covers up to her chin. The pleasant tiredness she felt made her snuggle down and smile happily as she thought of the past twenty-four hours or so.

She began to go back over each moment and as she did, something occurred to her. She was finally, at long last, coming into her own. She was finally happy.

It's about damn time, she thought.

She'd just started to drift off to sleep when she heard a frantic knock on her door. She sat up and looked at the time.

"Now who could that be?" The knocking came again and curious, she scurried out of bed and hurried to the door. A quick look through the peephole had her heart racing. Quickly, she unlocked the door and opened it wide. Jax rushed in and she leaped into his arms, wrapped her legs around his waist and her arms around his neck.

"What are you doing here?"

"I couldn't stay away. I don't want to stay away."

"Then don't." She leaned in to kiss him, starved for the taste of him. In a fevered rush for more, their lips met, and their tongues demanded. Their hands raced over each other's bodies, pulling and tugging clothing as they sought to feel each other skin to skin.

Jax kicked the door closed behind them and carried her into the living room. He sat with her on his lap and she could feel the hardening bulge in his pants. She found herself grinding against him and when she did, he grabbed her hips and began grinding back.

"Raise up, Charlie. Raise up and let me get these jeans off."

She did as he asked and he quickly removed the remainder of his clothes. Then he grabbed her and pulled her back down onto his lap. He cupped her breasts in his hands as if he were weighing them and tenderly rubbed his thumbs across her nipples until they were stiffened peaks. Taut and aching, his thumbs brushing against them added to her yearning.

She wanted him inside her and the more he played with her breasts the more she rubbed against him, grinding against his cock and wetting it with her arousal. With her arms around his neck, she ran her fingers through his thick, dark hair.

"I need you inside me, Jax. I don't understand it, but I can't seem to get enough of this. I can't get enough of you."

"Are you wet enough? Why don't you kiss me while I check?"

Once again their lips met and when he slipped his tongue back into her mouth and began to tangle with hers, he reached between them and slid two fingers into her wet heat. He rubbed them back and forth, coating them in her honeyed sweetness, and then transferred it to his cock, rubbing a circle around the tip. His pre-cum mixed with her arousal as he smoothed their lubrication down his hard length and he moaned his approval.

"More, Little Rabbit. More."

He reached between them again and this time, circled her clit. Her body jerked as he teased, and her pussy ached to be filled.

"Jax, I..."

"Cum for me. Let me hear you, Charlie."

She was already on the edge. The steady rhythm and repeating pattern he used as he played with her soon sent her climbing further, preparing her for that final peak and fall. She gripped his shoulders tightly to steady herself and moaned his name as she trembled.

"Jaxon...Oh, God!"

"That's it. Let it all out baby."

With a final circle around her clit, he gave a gentle pinch and she threw her head back and luxuriated in wave after wave of pleasure as her body bucked in a headrush of ecstasy. Then before she could come down, he grabbed her hips and slowly began to lower her pussy onto his hard cock.

"Oh, fuck, you're so damn tight!"

More. She wanted more and she needed it urgently. And without thought to anything other than filling the hollowness within, she sat fully on him, her pussy swallowing his length in one desperate gulp.

"Yes!" Charlie moaned as her instincts took over and she began to ride him. She loved the control she felt as she chose her speed, as she chose how deeply to let him in, sliding up and down his hard length like a pro. And when he gripped her hips and began meeting her thrusts with his own, she felt herself begin to climb that mountain of pleasure once more.

"Cum again for me, Little Rabbit. Cum on my cock..." His mouth latched onto one of her bouncing breasts, sucking on her nipple and flicking the tip with his tongue.

His wants, needs, and demands flowed through his words and the sound of his deep voice pushed her over the edge. The walls of her pussy began to spasm, her legs to tremble.

Simultaneously, they both moaned a single word. "Fuck..."

She swore the world stopped turning as she came, and when it started again, she realized he was speaking to her, coaxing her as she came down from her high.

"Relax, for me Charlie. I want to cum, need to cum, and your pussy is so tight, squeezing me so tightly, that I can't move."

She looked down into his incredible blue eyes and immediately her muscles began to loosen.

"You... You didn't cum?"

"Not yet."

Her initial shock at this revelation quickly disappeared as it dawned on her it was the perfect time to try out a skill she'd only read about. Taking her cue from all the steamy romance novels she'd ever devoured, she placed her finger against his lips and grinned at him.

"My turn."

Before he had a chance to stop her, she deftly raised up and off of his cock and lowered herself between his legs until her knees were resting on the floor and she was at eye level with his stiff erection. The bulbous head and stiff length of him glistened with her orgasm and the pronounced veins appeared to be pulsing as they waited for eruption.

"Holy shit, Charlie. Are you sure you're ready for this?"

Her answer for him was a barely perceptible nod as she wrapped her hands around him and began to explore. She caressed him softly before leaning forward and tentatively licking the tip. He gasped and she looked up at him, hoping she'd done something right to get such a reaction. When she saw his half-lidded eyes watching her intently, she knew his gasp had been one of pleasure.

She wanted to see his reaction. Without taking her eyes off him, she stuck her tongue out and softly licked again. When his eyes rolled back in his head, she realized just how much power she had over him. It was a heady feeling to know she could do so little and make him feel so good.

With that in mind, she sucked the tip into her mouth and ran her tongue around the head, flicking against the tip. She could taste herself on him and while she'd heard others lamenting over the taste of a woman's pussy, she didn't find it unpleasant at all.

She sucked herself off the tip and then went back for more. This time she took him in further before sucking back up his shaft. And when she looked up again and found his eyes glazed over, a tingle of pride and excitement shivered down her spine.

More. She wanted to give him more pleasure.

Instinct took over and she began to trace the prominent veins running up and down his cock. And when she took him in again she took him as far as she could go and hollowed out her cheeks as she sucked back up to the tip.

Then she did it again.

The moans and gasps of pleasure that continued to pour from Jax urged her on and soon she set up a rhythm. When she felt him place his hands on either side of her head and begin to softly run his fingers through her hair, it thrilled her.

"Oh, fuck... Charlie, that's fucking amazing."

That heady feeling floated around her once more, wrapping her in a shroud of excitement, and when he told her he was about to cum, she cupped his balls in her hand and gently encouraged him. She let them roll back and forth, and with her other hand, she pumped him. The combination of tonguing him, sucking him, and using her hands on him, sent him flying.

His cock stiffened beyond anything she'd ever felt before, the hard steel beneath the soft velvet of his skin making for an incredible dichotomy. It fascinated her when his hot cum began to spurt from his body. The salty essence was unexpected, but she decided instantly that she thoroughly enjoyed the taste.

And in her enjoyment, she swallowed everything he gave her.

Chapter Sixteen

Jax pulled Charlie's body against him and wrapped her in his arms as they stretched out on her bed and settled in for the night. His mind raced with what he wanted for the future, for their future, even as her breathing evened out and he felt her begin to slide into sleep. This, he thought. He just wanted this.

To be able to crawl into bed next to her every night. To have her in his arms whenever he wanted. To talk and laugh with her. To share new experiences with her as she finds her new path in life. To kiss her and make love with her until their bodies were blissfully exhausted.

Quite simply, he wanted forever.

How, he wondered, had he gone from a confirmed bachelor, happy with life on his own, to now questioning how he would continue to breathe if he wasn't near her? And how had all of it happened as quickly as it had? Life sure had a funny way of taking twists and turns.

When an alarm began to beep softly from his phone, the relaxed state he'd finally started to enter completely disappeared. He glanced down at Charlie as a sliver of moonlight shimmered through a slit in the gauzy curtain of her bedroom window, highlighting her form. It was as if he needed to check and make sure she was still there even though he could obviously still feel her sleeping next to him.

The alarm sounded again and he quickly and quietly disentangled himself and slipped out of bed. He grabbed his phone and brought up the alarm, then with a silent curse, made his way to the kitchen and grabbed a bottle of water to wet his suddenly parched throat.

It seemed he'd underestimated the private investigators on her case. They'd found her and were on their way.

They were coming to take her away from her new life and force her to return to a family who had never loved her and wanted to force her hand for their own nefarious interests. Well, he thought, he just wasn't going to let them.

They could try, but one way or another, she was staying with him. Never again would he let her feel as if she had nobody by her side, nobody to stand for her, and nowhere to turn.

They would face this together.

He looked at the time on his phone and grimaced. Part of him wanted to wake her, but he knew she needed rest. They didn't have much time, a day, maybe two at most. Decision made, he padded softly back into the bedroom and lay back down next to her. When she snuggled back against him, he wrapped her in his arms once more and held on tightly.

And with impending disaster looming over them, he closed his eyes and tried his best to sleep.

Charlie woke as she usually did, enjoying the hazy in-between of sleep and wakefulness. She stretched and arched her back, and when she felt the solid wall of man against her backside, her eyes popped open in surprise. His arms tightened around her and the hard steel of his morning erection pressed into the small of her back.

She smiled and bit her bottom lip as she began to playfully wiggle her ass against him.

"You're asking for trouble, Little Rabbit." His deep voice whispered groggily next to her ear as his warm breath brushed against the outer shell. Excited tingles of need cascaded down her spine and straight to her center, making her throb for him. She'd never known just how needy her body could get, but every time she was with Jax, her pussy gained a heartbeat and the liquid desire that accompanied it kept her wet and ready.

"Me? Trouble?" She grinned as she teased. "Just what kind of trouble are you talking about, Jaxon?"

Quickly, he shifted pressing her stomach into the mattress and pulling her knee up to an angle that left her spread open for him. He grabbed his cock and slid it in the wetness that slowly dripped from her, coating it as he prepared to enter her.

"This kind." He pushed inside her, filling her up with one long stroke. They both gasped as he held there, enjoying the tight heat she afforded.

"Oh, God, Jax! I'm so full."

"Oh, I've got more. You better hold on tight, Charlie."

He pulled out of her and slammed back inside. Moans of ecstasy filled the air as their bodies came together time and again. When he felt her body begin to tighten, to clamp down on his cock, he lost it. He grabbed a fistful of her hair and gently yanked her head back. His mouth dove for hers, his tongue claiming her and stroking inside her mouth in tandem with his cock as he fucked her.

Then with his mouth covering hers, his body filling her to overflowing, he reached between them and gently pinched her clit between his thumb and finger. With her body in overload and the breath backed up in her lungs, fireworks exploded within, from head to toe. As her eyes rolled back in her head from the bliss that overwhelmed her, she heard him whispering next to her ear.

"Breathe baby. Breathe."

When at last the orgasm finally passed, she collapsed on the bed. Her body felt liquefied as her muscles relaxed into a state of pleased exhaustion. As he pulled out of her and curled his large body around hers once more, he tucked her closely against him. She couldn't remember ever being so happy before.

She had fallen hard and fast for him and so far she was seriously enjoying every moment of her fall. She couldn't imagine her life being any better than it currently was.

Wrapped in a Jaxon cocoon, she quickly began to drift again, relishing the feel of his body and the sweet in-between of sleep and consciousness. But when Jax spoke again, her eyes popped open in alarm and her sleepiness faded quickly. She was instantly awake.

"I didn't want to have to tell you this, but you've been found, Charlie."

"What? What are you...?"

"I got an alert in the night. The investigators, maybe even your parents, are on their way to Ouray."

She tried to squirm out of his embrace, but he just wrapped her more tightly and held on until she stopped struggling. "What do you mean you got an alert? What did you do, Jax?"

"I told you I did some digging and laid a few false trails. When I did, I set up alerts so I would know if they got close. I wanted to be able to warn you, to protect you. Look. I know running seems like the logical thing to do right now, but you need to face them. You need to tell them you're not going to run anymore. You need to tell them they have no control over your life."

"They'll try to make me go back. They'll try to guilt me into returning. They'll play on my sympathies and as much as I want to think I've grown, changed, and wouldn't allow them to, I'm just uncertain if I would be able to fight them. I don't want to go back, Jax. I don't want to live where I'm not truly loved. I don't want to be a pawn in their schemes and I absolutely do NOT want to marry the man they've chosen for me. I'm happy here. For the first time in my life, I'm finally happy. I just can't go back."

"And you won't." He grabbed her chin and turned her head toward him so he could look into her eyes. "I'm not letting them take you from me."

Charlie rolled until she faced him and laid her head on his chest. The steady thud of his heart beating in his chest comforted her even as her mind raced. "You don't know what they're like, Jax. You don't know the lengths they'll go to make me return and do their bidding."

"I saw enough when I went digging. I've seen how they are and what they do. I wouldn't put anything past them." She saw his head tilt, his mouth lowering to hers and she met him halfway. The tenderness in his kiss helped to calm her further and when they separated, she sighed. "I'm afraid, Jax. I'm afraid they're going to find some way to make me leave."

"Listen to me. It isn't happening, You're not alone. I won't let you face them alone."

"But this isn't your fight."

"It is now. You haven't figured it out yet, have you?" He grinned at her and what she saw in his eyes made her heart skip a beat.

"Figured what out?"

"I'm in love with you, Charlie. And no matter how you feel about me, I'm not letting you do this by yourself. You can. I know you could. I have complete and total faith that you could. But the fact of the matter is, you don't have to, Little Rabbit. I'll stand beside you, support you, and let you handle your battles. But just say the word and I'll step in front of you and be your champion. Nobody is taking you from me."

Charlie wiped at the tears that formed in the corner of her eyes. "Jax. I..."

"Shh..." He pressed his finger to her lips. "It isn't that I don't want you to say it back – I do. But at the moment, your emotions are all over the place. Take some time. Let what I said settle. Right now, we need to figure out how we're going to handle things. Or, how you're going to handle things if you decide to take this on yourself."

She thought for a moment before she spoke again, "I think this might be an all-hands-on-deck situation. Do you think Logan will mind if we use the bar for the showdown?"

"Not at all. In fact, why don't we plan on meeting over there this afternoon before he gets busy?" Jax rolled out of bed and began to get dressed. "I'll get the guys there. You get the girls. And if you give me the go-ahead, I'll get Ryder looking into the legal end of things."

"Alright. It would be nice to have his help." She sat up and reached for her robe. "And Jax, I don't have to hold off on my end of that conversation. My emotions may be all over the place, but I know how I feel about you. I love you, Jaxon."

She stood and stepped into his embrace then wrapped her arms around his neck. "I love you and I'm so thankful that I passed out on your doorstep."

"Me too, Little Rabbit. Me too."

Early that afternoon Charlie, Jax, Logan, Sera, Ryder, and Alex sat around one of the back tables of Logan's Bar and discussed a plan of action.

Alex took a sip of her Coke and wrinkled her nose at the alcoholic beverages everyone else had in front of them. "You guys couldn't wait and do this when I'm off duty?"

"There's no time, and we're likely going to need the police here, so just drink your pop like a good little public servant, Alex." Ryder grinned as he picked up his beer and took a swig. The steely stare and middle finger Alex hurled in his direction made him chuckle even more as he took another swallow.

"I can't thank you all enough for coming together like this. For standing by me as I face this." Charlie looked around the table at her new friends and once again was struck by how lucky she was to have found each of them.

"Oh, honey! Of course, we're going to be with you – every step of the way. And Val is here in spirit since the hospital called her in to take a shift." Sera reached out and held Charlie's hands to comfort her as she spoke. "Let's figure this out so you can get on with your life."

"First things first," Jax stared steadily at the screen of his laptop as his fingers flew over the keyboard. "I've picked up the trail the investigators are leaving. They should be here sometime tomorrow afternoon, if not sooner. What I can't tell for sure is who they're bringing with them. I've been scanning the airlines, but haven't had anything pop up yet. However, I'm assuming with your parents' contacts they could easily have access to a private plane. That makes it a bit more difficult, though not impossible, to monitor."

Ryder spoke next. "I took a look at the paperwork for the trust that your great-great-grandparents set up. It is solid. Your parents can't touch it, no matter what they tell you. And you should receive your full payout when you turn twenty-six. Legally, they can't force you to do anything and they can't force you to turn over any money to them. I don't know whether your great-great grands saw the writing on the wall or had a crystal ball to look into, but they have you covered."

"So, it truly is going to come down to me being able to stand on my own two feet while I look my parents in the eyes and tell them to go to hell." Charlie gulped as anxiety began to snake its way through her nerve endings.

"You can do this. We know you can do it. We'll be with you, Charlie. And," Alex grinned, "if things get out of hand, I'll have my handcuffs with me. It's always good to have a police officer as a friend."

"Handcuffs. Probably used them last night, too." Ryder mumbled under his breath and cut his eyes to the side.

"What was that, Ry? Was that jealousy I heard there? Because it sounded like you might be jealous of my playmates," Alex teased.

"Not likely."

"The two of you need to stop. Today isn't about you and your fucked up non-relationship relationship," Sera scolded. Both Alex and Ryder rolled their eyes indignantly. "Let's get Charlie taken care of and then the two of you can do or not do whatever the hell you want."

"I'm going to put a sign up that I'm opening late tomorrow and I'm telling the crew to take a couple of hours." Logan reached for his phone and began to text.

"Oh, Logan." Charlie smiled, "You don't have to do that."

"I know I don't, but I don't mind. Once we have these people sent on their way, I'll open and we'll celebrate."

"Thank you." Charlie looked around the table at each of her new friends, her chosen family. "Thank all of you for all you've done and are doing for me. I can't tell you how much I appreciate it. I'm afraid to face them but I know it has to be done. I'm going to do it and it helps me so much to know you all will be here to support me."

"Oh, honey. There's no place else we'd rather be. Besides the fact that we all adore you, you seem to be making my brother pretty happy. I haven't seen him this relaxed in years!"

"He's making me pretty happy, too." Charlie blushed as she looked up at her lover and when the realization hit her that she did indeed have a lover, she couldn't keep the smile from her face.

"Don't forget," Jax began, "that thanks to our little side trip we have planned for first thing in morning, we have an out for you. If we have to do it, we will."

"Wait. What side trip? What are you two talking about?" Sera looked from Jax to Charlie and back to Jax.

"It's our ace in the hole, little sis, and we aren't playing that card until we have to."

Charlie looked to each of her friends and nodded, "Alright. Let's do this."

The next day, the group of friends met at the bar and waited. They were discussing last minute contingencies when Alex's phone rang. "I had all the calls to the station forwarded to my phone today. Give me just a minute."

"*Ouray Police Department. This is Officer Davis, how can I help you?*"

"*This is Garret Henley. I'm a retired detective who now works as a private investigator.*" Alex quickly put the call on speaker so everyone could hear.

"*Alright.*"

"*I'm calling because I'm looking for someone and I'm pretty sure she's in your area.*"

"*Well, we have quite a bit of tourist traffic here in Ouray.*"

"*I'm well aware. However, I'm pretty certain she's been in this area for a few weeks, closer to a month, maybe. Her name is Charlotte Abbingdon and her parents are worried sick about her and her welfare. She may be going by the name Charlie.*"

Jax nodded his head and mouthed to Alex to go ahead and get the investigator to the bar.

"Yes. Actually. I do know Charlie. In fact, I'm having lunch at Logan's Bar and she's here with a group of people. We're right in the middle of town. Is she in some kind of trouble?"

"No. No trouble. But as I said, her parents are worried and they've hired me to find her. I should be in Ouray within thirty minutes. I'll head that way and see if I can catch up to her."

"No worries, Mr. Henley. I'll stay here and keep an eye on her until you get here."

"Thanks. I'm on my way."

As Alex ended the call, Charlie got up and began to pace.

"I can do this."

Jax came up behind her and turned her to face him. "Of course you can. Just remember that you're not alone. You're never going to be alone again."

"I know." She laid her head on his chest and took a deep breath. "How did I ever get so lucky as to land on your doorstep?"

"I think the explanation is pretty simple. You're my fate. We were simply meant to be."

"Jax. That ace in the hole? I know you said to hold onto it, but I'm good with going ahead. Actually, I really want to do it."

"Are you sure?" Love, clear and evident, beamed from Jax's face.

"I love you, Jax. There's nobody else for me. There's no other place for me. I'm yours. And while I am absolutely going to stand up to them, I think it would be just splendid to throw that little bombshell at their feet before I send them on their way."

"Then let's do it!" Jax picked her up and spun in circles.

Chapter Seventeen

The swinging saloon doors to Logan's Bar flew open and four people walked through just as a cheer rang out and applause echoed throughout the bar. A tall man wearing a suit jacket which had seen better days stepped to the side and faded into the background to allow the trio with him a better view of their surroundings. As they made their presence known, the small group celebrating quieted and waited for the fireworks to begin.

It was obvious they were out of their element. Two men, one older, medium height and build, and the other much younger, taller, and somewhat athletic looking, carried an air of haughtiness as they peered down their noses. The clothing they wore spoke of high-end designers and perfectly tailored-to-fit materials.

The woman held much the same aura as the men next to her. It was obvious how she felt about standing in the middle of a bar which was much better suited to the local ranchers, small-town property owners, and weekend partygoers than to the "upper crust" of society they appeared to be.

The disgust on their faces was evident – the bar, its atmosphere and surroundings, as well as its occupants, were well beneath their standards.

Charlie spoke first. "Mother. Father. What a surprise. And I see you've brought Andrew with you, as well."

"Charlotte," the woman began, "if you're done with all this foolishness then it's time to gather your belongings and return home. Andrew and the Montgomerys are quite anxious to begin preparing for your wedding."

"I am home and I'm not going anywhere with you. And I am most certainly not marrying him." Charlie pointed at the younger man who stood taking in the scene before him.

With his face turning red and anger apparent, her father took three steps toward her. "Don't be ridiculous, Charlotte. I've had quite enough of your acting out."

"Sir. If I may?" Andrew stepped forward at the same time he inclined his head toward her father. "Charlotte. Do I need to remind you of your obligations? Our families entered into an agreement a long time ago. It's now time for us to complete that transaction. And as the fiance of a future senator, I need you to remember your place and act with the utmost decorum. Your unseemingly display of obstinance and childishness is going to take quite a bit of time, money, and effort to cover. Please don't make this any more difficult than it already is. It will not end well for you if you do."

Jax rushed forward and grabbed Andrew by the lapels of his jacket, jerking him off his feet. "Did you just threaten her?"

Charlie's mother gasped and covered her mouth in shock. "Oh dear!"

"Put him down! Put him down at once!" Charlie's dad took a step forward to try to intervene. Alex cleared her throat and with her hand on her taser, walked forward until she was in the center of the room. When Charlie's dad saw the police presence, he stopped in his tracks.

"Who the hell are you?" Andrew questioned as he struggled against the steely grip Jax had on him, "Remove your hands before I have you arrested!"

Jax grinned devilishly at the man struggling within his grasp. "Go ahead and try."

Charlie shook her head. "It's alright, Jax, put him down."

"Yes, Jax," Andrew all but spit out the name in disgust, "do put me down."

With his feet hovering a couple of inches off the floor, Jax dropped him and gave him a slight push – a warning of things to come if he so much as tried to put his hands on Charlie. Once Andrew was free of Jax's grasp, he brushed at his suit jacket as if just having Jax touch him had dirtied him in some way.

"Gentlemen. Ma'am." Alex looked back and forth between the late arrivals, "I do believe Charlie made it pretty clear she doesn't want to leave and if I'm reading the undercurrents in her statement correctly, she more specifically doesn't want to go anywhere with you – with any of you." Alex looked to Charlie for confirmation, "Do I have the gist of the situation, Charlie?"

"Absolutely, Officer Davis."

"Charlotte Grace Abbingdon. What has gotten into you?"

Charlie looked at her mother and with courage she'd never felt before and suggestive mischievousness, answered, "My husband."

"Husband?!" Charlie's father roared with indignation. "What on earth are you talking about?"

"Mother. Father." Charlie wrapped her arms around Jax's waist. "Let me introduce you to your new son-in-law,

Jaxon Payne. As of five minutes ago, I am no longer Charlotte Grace Abbingdon. I am now Mrs. Charlie Payne."

"This is preposterous." Charlie's parents looked unbelieving at the group who stood before them.

"You...defiled my fiance?" Disgust wove its way through Andrew's words as he looked Jaxon up and down.

Jax started to speak but Charlie stopped him. "I never was nor ever will be your fiance. I was never asked to marry you and certainly never consented to marrying you. I suggest you go home, Andrew. Find someone else to be your dutiful little wife."

"Why I ought to..." Andrew took a step forward in anger, reaching for Charlie, and immediately a look of regret flashed across his face as Jax doubled up his fist and plowed it into the man's nose. Andrew went flying backward and landed with a thud as he crashed into a nearby table and chair.

Jax shook his head in disbelief. "I warned you." Blood began to pour from the man's nose.

"You've just made a huge mistake. I'll press charges." Andrew reached in his pocket for a handkerchief to mop up the blood. "Officer," he looked toward Alex, "I want this man arrested."

"Well, now," Alex grinned and shrugged her shoulders, "I don't believe I can do that. I was witness to the entire altercation and you were the aggressor. Jax was simply defending his wife. If anyone belongs in jail, that would be you."

Charlie's mother gasped, "Well, I never..."

"No, ma'am, I don't suppose you have, which explains so much." Alex raised her eyebrow as she turned and rejoined the crew standing behind Charlie and Jax.

"Charlotte!" Her father began waving his hands, incredulous of the situation before him, "This is preposterous. You're making a huge mistake. This man will never be able to provide you with the life you're accustomed to."

"He already gives me everything I need and want. I've never needed the money, the mansion, the clothes, the servants, and I most certainly never needed a place in society. If you truly believe that, then you don't have even a modicum of knowledge of who your daughter truly is." Charlie looked at her parents with pity.

"Do you really think," Charlie's mother, nose in the air with haughtiness, looked at Jax, "you're going to want her to stay with you? You'll be bored with her in no time. How on earth could you possibly want someone like her? She has no social skills, though goodness knows we tried. You'll regret taking her on. We arranged this marriage because we knew she would never actually attract a man of good social standing on her own. We've done nothing but look out for her best interest. She'll be nothing but a burden to you."

"You truly don't know your daughter at all. She is the most wonderful blessing of my life and I'm proud to call her my wife. Your daughter has made me the happiest man in the world and it is my intention to give her everything she's ever needed and never had. And yes, I have the means to care for her, not only emotionally and physically, but financially, as well." Jax kissed the top of her head and then smiled at her parents.

"I have no idea what you're talking about. My daughter has never wanted for anything." Her father's face turned beet red and anger radiated from every pore.

Charlie looked at her parents with pity. "You gave me a roof over my head. You gave me food, an education, clothing, lessons. You gave me basic necessities that were coated in the financial status of the lap of luxury. You never gave me love. You never gave me caring and tenderness. You were never there for me when I needed to be held and tended to. You gave me anxiety, depression, and emotional upsets that nobody should ever encounter, much less a young child. All I've ever been to you was a means to an end. Well, I will not be that means for you and you will face whatever end comes your way without me being your pawn or scapegoat. I'm a grown woman. I'm a married woman. And I'm happy here with my friends, my true family, and now, my husband."

"This marriage is a farce and it should be annulled." Her mother's voice began to tremble the tiniest bit as the realization of their future began to make itself known.

Ryder stepped forward, "This marriage is perfectly legal. My clients - I'm their attorney, by the way - went to the county courthouse just this morning and got their marriage license. As I'm duly authorized to perform marriage ceremonies, I've just done so, and their marriage certificate was signed mere moments before you walked in the door. Jax and Charlie are legally wed."

Jax kissed the top of Charlie's head before smiling mischievously at her parents. "It seems that your unscrupulous plans for your daughter have been thwarted."

"You have the choice to either be happy for me and Jax, and us maintaining a semi-cordial relationship, or you can walk out of my life and never look back. I'm fine with either door you choose." Charlie looked back and forth between her mother and father and smiled from ear to ear as she waited to see what they would do.

"This isn't the end of this, young lady." Her father, fists balled in anger, took a step toward her. When he did, Jax stepped in front of her and crossed his arms over his massive chest – a barrier of protection once again for the woman he loved.

"It's alright, Jax. He won't hurt me." Charlie stepped forward so she was seen once again. "We're done here."

"You haven't heard the last of us."

"Let me just go on record for my client on one more matter. She is not nor will she ever be obligated to pay you any amount of money and you are not ever getting your hands on any of the funds from her trust. It is my understanding that this amazing woman has a birthday coming up and she will be receiving the full payout of that trust on that date. You can rest assured that I will be looking out for my client's best interest helping her to set up trusts of her own and facilitating some financial planning to ensure she, her husband, and any future progeny are well taken care of." Ryder smirked as the realization that they'd lost their game showed on their faces – shocked disbelief under indignant self-righteousness.

"In short," Jaxon continued, "she is ours and we will always do what's best for her."

"If we're done here," Sera broke in, "I'm ready to have some wedding celebrations!"

"Mother. Father. Thank you for stopping by on my wedding day, but if you're not here to congratulate me and my husband, you can see yourselves out – out of the bar, out of Ouray, out of my life. Andrew," she turned to face the man still blotting at the blood on his face and clothes, "I hope whoever you end up marrying is much more suited to your expected role of demure wife. I wish you well."

When the unwelcomed visitors made their exit, another round of cheers filled the bar. Charlie looked up into Jaxon's face and grinned with happiness.

"I did it. We did it."

"We did, Little Rabbit. More importantly, you did. You were magnificent!" Jax leaned down to kiss her and when he did, he picked her up and hugged her tightly. "Wife. I love you."

"Husband. I love you more." Suddenly a thought crossed her mind and curious, she turned to Jax for an explanation. "What exactly did you mean by your statement you have the financial means to care for me?"

Jax chuckled, "My business does very well for itself, Charlie. Between what I bring in and the investments I've made over the past few years or so, we won't ever have to worry about money."

"You mean..."

"I mean we have more money than we'll ever spend, Little Rabbit. Not only that but if we ever decide to add to our family and expand our nest, our children will be set, too."

"I don't know what to say to that."

"You don't have to say anything. Just know that I'm always going to take care of you." Jax looked around and grinned at their friends who were passing around drinks and talking loudly. "You realize we're going to have to do this all again, right? The wedding?"

"Oh, I'm planning on it. I want it all, Jax."

"Well, then, your husband is going to see to it that your every dream, wedding or otherwise, becomes reality."

"I keep asking myself how I got so lucky as to land on your doorstep, but the answer is simple: yuanfen – a firm belief that destiny or fate plays a part in bringing two lovers together. You're my destiny, Jax."

"And you're my fate."

"Forever?" She looked hopefully into his eyes.

"Forever and always."

Epilogue

Six months later...

"Charlie! Charlie! Get in here!" Jax looked from screen to screen and shook his head. The proverbial shit had finally hit the fan. He hated that the news he was about to share might hurt her, but she needed to know.

Charlie rushed into his office, mild panic on her face. "I'm here. What? What's going on?"

"It just popped up on the news. Your parents filed for bankruptcy. Two hours later they were arrested. In fact, a whole bunch of people in their inner circle have been arrested."

Jax held his hand out to her and she went to him, sinking onto his lap as she, too, stared at the screens.

"Embezzlement, larceny, forgery, misappropriation of public and private property – the list goes on and on. From the looks of it, each of the charges has multiple infractions. It's bad. If they're found guilty they could face many years in prison."

He looked at her with concern. She hadn't said a word as he'd filled her in. Now she sat staring at the screens reading the news blurb over and over with a look he couldn't quite put a name on. After a few moments, a corner of her mouth began to kick up into a smile.

"Good."

"Are you alright, Little Rabbit?"

"I'm more than alright, Jax. This is what I wanted. This is what we wanted."

"I know, but seeing it actually happening? Well, I wasn't sure how you would feel about it if and when the time came." Jax smoothed his hand down her back as he comforted her.

"Indubitably, I'm happy. They're getting what they deserve. It's past time for the abuse and fraud that has been carried from generation to generation in my family to stop. I'm glad it is finally ending with me. I'm glad I had a hand in making this happen."

"Taking everything to the Attorney General's office so they had a case built and a plan in place was smart. Handing them a can of worms and giving our statements took so much courage. I'm so proud of you for taking all these steps."

"It needed to be done."

"It did. I know we've talked about the possibility before, but I just want to remind you that you may have to take the stand one day."

"I know. I can do it if I have to. They need to answer for all they've done, all they were prepared to do. If I can have a hand in stopping this vicious cycle, I'll be pleased."

"You're amazing."

"Thank you, Jax." She wrapped her arms around his neck and placed a kiss on his lips.

"For what?"

"For encouraging me. For standing beside me. For being l'amour de ma vie – the love of my life."

"I'll always stand beside you. There's no place I'd rather be." He paused and smiled sexily at her. "Almost no place I'd rather be. I mean on top of you? Behind you? Any position as long as it gets me inside you. I'm good with them all." The teasing light in his eyes was instantly reflected back at him from hers.

She smacked his arm playfully. "You're insatiable."

"I am. How about we try one of those positions right now?"

"Hmm..." She turned and straddled his lap. "I think," she grinned, "it's time to see if we can come up with a new position."

"Oh, Little Rabbit. I do love the way you think. Everything about you turns me on, but that mind of yours? It gets me every time."

"Say it with me, Jax. Sapiosexual."

He laughed loudly and when he did, the dog came running from the other room, barking happily.

"Alright! Alright! You win. No matter how it sounds, I'll agree. I'm a sapiosexual. Now, let's see if that brilliant mind of yours can figure out what I'm thinking."

She giggled as she reached for the zipper on his jeans. "Oh, I know. Believe me, Jax, I know..."

The end.

About the Author

Dawn Love

Dawn Love was born in Mayfield, Kentucky, and spent the first twenty-six years of her life there. Always a creative person and an avid reader, she began writing stories for her own entertainment as a teen, and her love of writing continued to grow into adulthood. She now lives on her

50-acre farm on the Delmarva Peninsula. A mother of two, she spends her free time creating the characters and stories of her fantasies. She also writes an internationally read blog where she gives her readers a glimpse into the craziness of her day-to-day life, her mind, and all that the world throws her way.

To stay up-to-date with all things Dawn, join her newsletter family! And just for signing up, you'll get access to her newsletter-exclusive digital book, Truth, Lies & Fantasies!

https://dawnlovebooks.com/contact/

More By Dawn Love

Meet the Cassidy Brothers!

These sexy, single brothers may not be looking for their happily ever after, but fate has other ideas. Join Cade, Cameron, Colton, Calvin, and Colby as their destinies are revealed!

The Cassidy Brothers

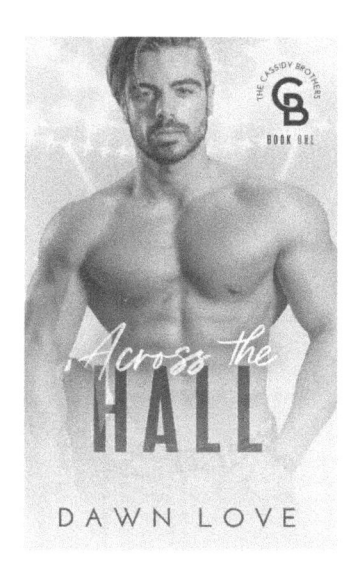

Across the Hall

He fell in love when he was eight years old. His summer vacation had led to a childhood crush that he'd never forgotten. Though he didn't realize it, he'd looked for her in every woman he'd dated. She'd fallen in love, too. The lonely little girl she'd been had found a new friend, making for her best vacation ever. She's all grown up now but still lonely, perhaps more so than ever. A walk on the beach will change both their worlds forever.

Across the Road

She fled the city searching for a new life. Leaving all she'd ever known behind her had been a snap decision, but if things go her way, it will be the best decision she will have ever made. He was looking for love without even realizing it. When she walked into his bar seeking a job, he had no idea she would be the love he was waiting for. They can only have their happy ending if her disastrous past doesn't track her down and destroy the life they want to build together.

Across the Lane

He's the bad boy of the family who hides his heart of gold behind a tough exterior, a leather jacket, and a Harley. He works hard and plays harder. He's known for his wild and wicked ways, but all he really wants is love. She is only in town for the summer and plans to make the most of it. She's had her future laid out for as long as she can remember, and if her plans come together, she'll make a huge leap toward fulfilling her dreams. Their chance meeting causes sparks to fly and desires to soar.

Across the Field

Calvin has dreamed of playing in the big leagues his entire life. He works hard, trains hard, and plays harder. Having watched his older brothers falling in love and starting families, he determines that he just isn't about that kind of life. Being free to play the field romantically and sexually, while he plays the field for a living, is what it's all about in his book. Jillian has loved sports for as long as she can remember and the camera loves Jillian. She's smart, quick, and witty - everything a major sports broadcast needs to keep the fans interested and on their toes. She loves being single and has no intentions of settling down any time soon. It only takes one night for their carefully laid plans to get hit out of the park.

Across the Miles

Colby Cassidy is a player. He's always been a player and feels no need to change his wicked ways. The women he gets involved with know the score and endgame. He's always excelled at whatever he's done and his sexual exploits are no different. Over the past few years he's watched his brothers fall, one by one, head over heels into the bliss of love and happily ever after. Being last-man-standing has him constantly looking over his shoulder and worrying that it's only a matter of time before he finds himself on the ledge. Will he jump, fall, or be pushed into what he never knew he wanted? Juliette Tate's life belongs to the stage. Years and years of ballet has trained her body hard for the rigors of the dance world and she's finally started to make a name for herself in the Big Apple. When she suddenly finds herself in a tight spot, she does what she has to do to scrape by. She never thought her dance skills would be used quite the way they are, but she's making the most of it. At least she is until her secret is discovered and the one man she has a hard time saying no to, steps in with an indecent proposal. Will fate tear them apart or push them together?

Looking for romantic suspense? Dive into the Mountain Mayhem series and meet Blaze and Lexi!

Mountain Haven

They say when life hands you lemons, make lemonade. But for Lexi Lane, life didn't hand her those lemons. Instead, they were hurled from a grenade launcher. It's been almost five years since her world detonated around her, and she's moved on from that sour time in her life - or so she thinks. Hiding out in the mountains of West Virginia has given her the solitude she's needed to survive, but surviving is all she's done. When a stranger crashes into her life, will she finally be able to open herself to feel again? To love again? Michael "Blaze" Blaisure has devoted his life to righting some of the wrongs in the world. Part of a covert military unit, he has traveled from country to country and seen the pits of hell first-hand. After witnessing more death and despair than his heart and soul could take, he makes the decision to change directions and choose a new path. But will that path lead to acceptance and forgiveness for his part in tragedy and death? All it takes is a mountain, a storm, and the hand of fate to open their eyes to new horizons. But when danger appears, will it separate them, or bring them closer than ever?

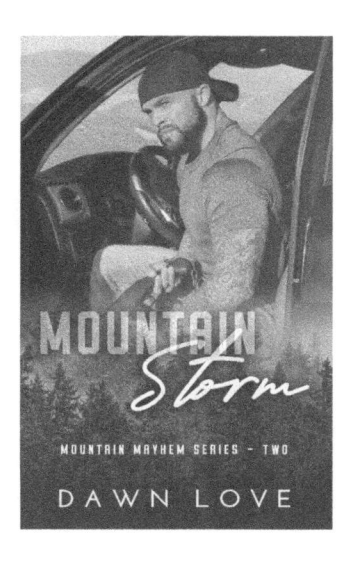

Mountain Storm

They say you must weather the storms to find a rainbow. Michael "Blaze" Blaisure and Lexi Lane have endured some of life's hardest trials and are finally beginning to see clear skies. Now, they're ready for the next phase of their lives to begin. A new career path and a new venture may be just what they need to move forward. As they take those steps together, they are unaware of the danger lurking around the next corner. When the past rears its ugly head, they must face some of the most turbulent storms of their lives. Will they survive the landslide headed their way? Or will fate rip them apart?

Welcome to Canyon Creek!

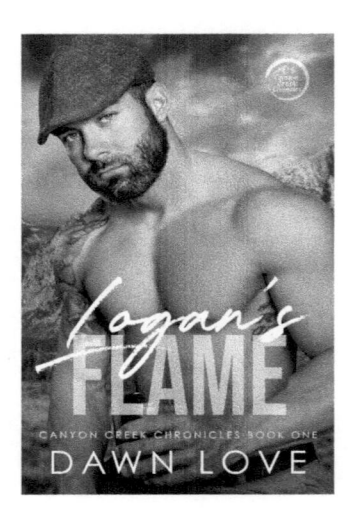

Logan's Flame

Falling in love with your best friend's sister may not be taboo to everyone. For Logan Grant, it's simply unthinkable. A man of his word, Logan would never break a pact he made, no matter how much heart-wrenching agony he suffers each time he thinks of the woman of his dreams. Sera was, is, and always will be the one who owns him – heart, mind, body, and soul. Staying true to his word is becoming harder and harder the more time they spend together. As the sexual tension between them grows, so does his need to be with her. A best-selling author, Seraphina Matthias has decided to take her research to the next level, and she knows there's only one man she wants to fill the role of muse and partner in discovery. Close friends, Logan has always been there to catch her as she stumbles through life. Although she's never really thought about him sexually or romantically, she knows she trusts nobody else to help her with her research – even if he is completely unaware of her intentions. Will Logan be able to stay true to himself and honor his agreement while his heart's desire begins to play a wicked game? Will Sera's secrets cause her to lose his trust and friendship? His love?